Apache Tears

Also by Tom Diamond

RIMFIRE

Apache Tears

Tom Diamond

This is a work of fiction based on historical persons and occurrences with dramatization of characters.

Apache Tears

Chapter image "Apache Head-dress and Boots" by W. Roberts from John Bartlett, 1854, John Carter Brown Library.

ISBN-13: 978-0-944551-79-0
ISBN-10: 0-944551-79-3

First Edition
9 8 7 6 5 4 3 2 1

Beaverhead Lodge Press
H. C. Box 446
Burnt Cabin, Beaverhead
Winston, New Mexico 87943

Publishing Assistance by

Book Publishers of El Paso
1055-B Humble Place
El Paso, Texas 79915
(915) 778-6670
www.bookpublishersofelpaso.com

In Memory of

Vine Deloria

valiant warrior

trusted advisor

faithful friend

Apache Headdress and Moccasin
by W. Roberts (John Bartlett, 1854)

Foreword

Throughout the Southwest, small obsidian flakes can be found. They are called "Apache Tears". Hard, sharp, and brittle, they symbolize the bitter legacy of the Apache Nation's fight to maintain its sovereignty.

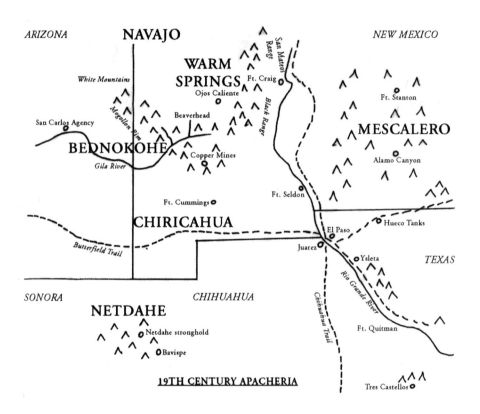

ARIZONA   **NAVAJO**   *NEW MEXICO*

**WARM
SPRINGS**   Ft. Craig

White Mountains

San Mateo Range

Ojos Caliente

Ft. Stanton

Black Range

San Carlos Agency

Mogollon Rim

Beaverhead

MESCALERO

BEDNOKOHE

Copper Mines

Alamo Canyon

Gila River

Ft. Cummings

Ft. Seldon

CHIRICAHUA

Hueco Tanks

Butterfield Trail

El Paso

TEXAS

Juarez

Ysleta

SONORA   *CHIHUAHUA*

NETDAHE

Rio Grande River

Netdahe stronghold

Chihuahua Trail

Ft. Quitman

Bavispe

19TH CENTURY APACHERIA

Tres Castellos

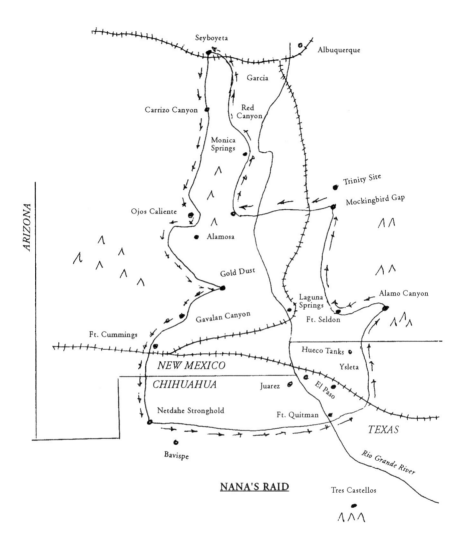

NANA'S RAID

Apache Tears

CHAPTER ONE

Disaster at Tres Castillos

Lozen's horse shied from a coarse clump of yucca while sounding a snort of warning. Lozen sensed what was troubling her mount and glanced down at the clump of yucca but could see no sign of a snake.

She turned in her saddle. Making the sign of a snake, she called back to the next rider, "Be careful, there is a rattlesnake in the yuccas."

Lozen rode on, slumping forward in the saddle, hoping to be able to close her eyes and get a little sleep. The Apaches had been riding since dawn, putting distance between themselves and the 11th Cavalry under Colonel Grierson, and were now deep into Mexico and felt that they were safe from attack by the Buffalo Soldiers.

The last three months had been hell for the Warm Springs Apache band under Victorio. They had been harried throughout the Black Range, the Gila Basin, the Sacramentos and the Guadalupes by the Americans. The only respite was to dart south into Mexico, where, unknown to the Apaches, General Terrazas had been assembling a major force to end the Apache depredations.

Ahead of Lozen was the main body consisting of 300 braves,

women, and children. Preceding them was a group of 20 braves acting as the advance party, being led personally by Victorio, the brother of Lozen. Lozen and 10 other women were bringing along the pack animals loaded with cooking utensils, skins, food, and ammunition. When Lozen turned to warn the others about the snake, she had seen a cloud of dust on the horizon, and knew that it was kicked up by Nana and 20 warriors who were guarding the rear. She looked ahead to see if there was a telltale plume of dust being raised by the main party but was unable to see through the setting sun's brilliance.

As she slouched in the saddle, trying to rest, she let her eyes close. She drowsed while vividly imagining her home at Ojos Caliente between the Wahoos and the San Mateos mountains at the box of Canada Alamosa. The Ojos Caliente rancheria was the summer headquarters of her band, the Chihenne, called by the Americans "Warm Springs" Apaches. The Chihenne occupied all of the Black Range but a portion of them summering near Santa Rita had long been in the process of becoming a distinct band. Even before the death of Mangas Colorado, the two groups had operated under different chiefs.

Lozen and her brother, the great Chief Victorio, had been brought up at Warm Springs, the children of a Chihenne woman who had married a Bedonkohe man. Their father had been born fifty miles to the west on the middle fork of the Gila River in the same rancheria where Geronimo had been born. The Bedonkohe were closely related to the Chihenne Apache and the two groups had once been a single band. Lozen's father was a descendant of Mahko, the great Bedonkohe Chief who led all of the Southern Apaches many years earlier.

Lozen's mother was the daughter of Cuchillo Negro, a Chihenne Chief who had been murdered at Janos, Old Mexico along with other Chihenne and Bedonkohe including the wife and children of Geronimo.

When the Warm Springs Chihenne were uprooted from the Ojo Caliente reservation in 1876 and sent to San Carlos, Lozen was

35 years old and the only woman in her band who had never married. Victorio had frequently talked to her about the need to be married and had suggested promising warriors as possible mates. Whenever these discussions came up, Lozen would energetically demand, "Brother do not talk to anyone's parents about marriage, I refuse to be bought or sold as chattel."

This was just as well, for the young men were all intimidated by Lozen's athletic abilities and her strong personality. It had been obvious from the days when Lozen was a toddler that she was different from the other Apache maidens. While the young girls made mud figures to play with and played the other girls' games she was busy making bows and practicing the hunting games of the boys'. No boy her age could outrun her or put her down in a wrestling match. Her parents strongly disapproved of her preferences at play but the minute their backs were turned, she would cast aside the feminine pursuits and compete with the boys head on.

Lozen's horse came to an abrupt stop and she was instantly awake. She saw that one of the mule packs had come loose and was spilling its cargo. It was the pack that contained the ammunition, the most important provision carried by the mules. Lozen got off her horse and called to two others, "Come help me with this pack."

She supervised the repacking, as ammunition meant life or death to the Apaches. Once the pack was secure, Lozen vaulted back into her saddle, not using the stirrups, but leveraging herself, her hands on the pommel and an elbow on the cantle.

As the little group started out, Lozen noted the sun was almost on the horizon and felt that they would reach their destination at Tres Castillos within an hour. She again closed her eyes and dozed. A smile formed on her lips as she recalled the constant urgings of Victorio to permit him to find her a husband. She always told him, "I am not interested. None of the boys appeal to me. I don't want any of them."

He always remonstrated with her saying, "But you must. You can't be an unmarried woman in the Apache tribe. We need the women to have our children and you need a husband to provide for you and your children."

After she had turned twenty with Victorio having kept up his insistence, one night, by the campfire, she told him that ever since her initiation to womanhood, she had had recurring dreams in which she returned to the sacred mountain and was visited in the cave by Ussen in the form of a giant animal whose name could not be spoken. Victorio instantly knew to whom she referred and did not press her to disclose its identity. "Ussen," she said, "told me that I was not to marry and live the same as other Apaches. Instead I must be prepared for a life of sacrifice in ways that will be revealed." Lozen drifted into sleep and in her dreams remembered her girlhood.

After telling Victorio why she had such an aversion to marriage, he let her be. This did not end, however, the rumors and speculation rampant in the community with regard to her sexual preferences. There was much whispering that this Lozen was one of those women who could not be broken to the hand of man but liked other women instead. The Apaches knew that every once in a while a woman was born who had these inclinations but, normally, the peer pressure was so great that they eventually married and were forced into the traditional feminine role pattern.

Once in a while, a woman would be so ingrained towards the same sex that she would be expelled from the band and forced to exist on her own. Of course, this often meant death because an individual, in particular a woman with less strength and hunting skills than a man, could not survive alone in the fierce environment in which the Apaches lived.

With Victorio as the Chief of the Warm Springs, none dared suggest that Lozen be forced from the tribe. On the other hand, there was growing appreciation among the Warm Springs that, indeed, here was a gifted woman and that perhaps it was intended that she be alike only to herself. There was no doubt that her power was equal to anyone's. The aura of specialness that always surrounded her was made more acute by the fact that her power had not been seen since the great Chief Mahko had died. If the ankle biters had had their way and Lozen had left the Chihennes, any of the other

Apache bands would have gladly taken her in so that they could benefit from her great gift.

Lozen's drowsing was shattered by a virtual explosion inside her mind. She visualized the horizon on fire and shots ringing out on every side. Lozen screamed as she opened her eyes, "Our people are being attacked! Our people are being attacked!"

Everyone gathered around her, knowing that some terrible thing was occurring. Lozen immediately sent one of the younger women who was on the fastest horse to find and alert Nana that the main party was in trouble. She and the woman abandoned the pack animals and raced towards Tres Castillos.

As they dashed to catch up with the main party the sun completed its journey and the light began to fade. After half an hour they were only three miles from the shallow lake at the foot of the Tres Castillos formation. At that distance they could see a giant fire burning and hear the muffled sound of rifle fire. On they raced, with Lozen in the lead, until they were about a mile from the scene of conflict.

Lozen reigned in and held up her little group while she surveyed the situation. Other fires were burning and she could see the flash of gunfire from pockets of resistance. She debated what to do. *I have the only rifle. All others only have knives. What can we do? We have stumbled into hell.* She commanded the women, "Wait here while I reconnoiter."

Half a mile from the scene of the tragedy she could tell from the diminishing fire that the end was near. She stopped her horse. Horrified, she could see bands of Mexican cavalry chasing Indians through the chaparral, spearing and shooting them. There were only two pockets of resistance left. She sat on her horse, trembling. Shortly, the firing stopped and she could hear the shouts of the Mexicans as they began to celebrate their victory. She wheeled her horse and dashed back to where the women were waiting. Excitedly she shouted, "Stragglers are trying to escape the Mexicans. Spread out and intercept any Apaches and direct them to our next rendezvous at Cerro de Barrison."

Seventeen women and young children were all that escaped the terrible massacre at Tres Castillos. General Terrazas had done what the combined might of the United States and Mexico, coupled with every group of militia along the border, had been unable to accomplish for six years. The great Victorio was dead. And while a Tarahumara man claimed to have been the one that shot the great Chief, Lozen knew from her visions that he had, after using all his ammunition, perished on his own knife.

As the women and children were intercepted, they were led towards the rendezvous site. Lozen, in the meantime, had picked up the pack mules and with quick thinking saved their supplies. As she was taking the mules to the cave for refuge, Nana's party came rushing up. They stopped and Lozen related what had happened. Nana divided his warriors and directed half of them to escort the pack mules and stragglers to the sanctuary while he went forward with a small group to personally survey the carnage. He was not able to get as close as Lozen had but he could see the fires and could see the Mexican cavalry still searching for survivors. He was about three quarters of a mile from the scene when he heard a volley of shots followed by complete silence. Instinctively, the old man knew the Mexicans were executing captives and, with revulsion, he turned and retreated with his men to save what he could of the remnants of the Warm Springs band with one thought in mind, *I must do everything I can to save the survivors. We will need every man, woman, and child.*

Of the three hundred Apaches that perished that day, almost all were Warm Springs. There were a few Mescaleros and two Lipans with those that had joined Victorio before the final battle.

The day after the massacre, three young warriors that Nana had sent out to determine the position of the Mexicans, reported that there were Apache prisoners, women and young children, being marched towards Chihuahua. They also reported that there were cavalry contingents spread out in every direction looking for the remainder of Victorio's band. Nana felt that it was too dangerous to wait any longer at the rally point and immediately divided the force into three groups, sending them in different directions but all heading towards a final rendezvous in the Black Range.

Nana left one brave behind to tell other stragglers where they had gone so they would know where the next rendezvous point was. This was one of the strategies that had enabled the Apaches to be so successful in their fight with the white-eyes. They always had contingency plans ready and rallying points selected in advance if, for any reason, they were suddenly attacked or they were bested in battle. This kept them organized and able to regroup and endure the inevitable setbacks.

Lozen accompanied Nana from Mexico passing just east of El Paso, Texas. The small party traveled only at night and carefully hid the sign of their passage. The survivors of the Tres Castillos massacre finally assembled in a hidden glade south of Ojos Caliente. There were only eighty people and just fifteen of them were warriors. Nana had sent messengers throughout the Black Range and the Gila Basin in the Mogollon Mountains with instructions to contact all Chihenne Apaches and have them assemble at the rendezvous point.

All had been driven to the limit of their endurance. In their first night of relative safety, the enormity of the tragedy of Tres Castillos weighed heavily on Lozen. In addition to the great Victorio she had lost all of her immediate family. She slept fitfully in great anguish and when her sleep deepened, her thoughts defensively turned to the happy days of her youth and, in particular, her passage to womanhood and the great visions visited on her by Ussen. Her wandering mind drifted back to the day she had become a woman.

Apache Tears

CHAPTER TWO

The Blue Mountains

On that eventful day, excitement was running high in the village as the Chihenne band prepared to leave their summer headquarters and go down into the barrancas of the Blue Mountains of Old Mexico. They had been invited by their cousins, the Netdahe, to winter with them and share a reunion of their closely-knit bands. The Bedonkohe band to their west on the headwaters of the Gila, were included in the invitation and everyone was looking forward to the trip. The younger people were extremely excited because they knew that at this type of gathering, marriages would be arranged as it was desirable to marry into other bands to keep each group invigorated. Lozen was particularly excited because she wanted to meet other Apache youngsters and test her athletic skills.

The Warm Springs girls shunned Lozen because she was so strong and powerful and the boys were embarrassed for Lozen to best them at their games of running and wrestling. Perhaps in the Netdahe, who were known for their physical prowess, she would find young girls like herself who were athletes and with whom she could compete.

That morning Lozen went to the largest of the Warm Springs to take her bath with the other girls. The boys had been permitted their opportunity to bathe an hour earlier and now, by tradition, were barred from the pool and environs. Lozen eagerly slipped from her tunic and plunged into the warm pool, swimming rapidly to the other side. She was a proficient swimmer, not because she had large bodies of water in which to practice but because she practiced her heart out whenever she found any water deep enough and wide enough across to permit a few strokes.

She swam rapidly back and forth a dozen times and was resting on the opposite bank when she glanced down and noticed the water between her legs was reddening. She thought, *I have cut myself on a rock.*

She felt for a wound. There was none. It then occurred to her, *I have reached womanhood, and the bleeding cycle has begun.*

All Apache girls had been told from childhood that some day their function would change and they would endure a passage to womanhood and assume their roles as mothers, teachers, and providers for their people.

Lozen, in high excitement, swam back across the pool then quickly put on her tunic. Leaving the other girls at play in the water she ran to her mother's wickiup. She rushed inside and, even though her father was present, blurted out the news, "The change is upon me."

With this announcement, her father quickly left the wickiup and her mother confirmed that, indeed, Lozen had reached the point of change in her life.

Later that afternoon, Lozen's father conferred with the elders of the tribe including Lozen's brother Victorio who had just the past month been elected Principal Chief of the northern Chihenne. It was decided immediately that the trip must be delayed to permit Lozen to complete the obligatory ceremony.

Lozen had only two short days to prepare herself. Lozen's mother and the other women repeatedly schooled her about what her duties must be as she underwent her ordeal of puberty. They didn't have to remind her that an arduous task lay before her. For years she had known that the time would come when she would be alone in the wilderness for four days and that it was crucial she do so with purity of mind and body. Lozen was pure and was ready for this spectacular event in her life although she was fearful that she would not be able to rise to the expectation that everyone had of her.

Lozen's father, mother, and brother accompanied her. They were all mounted, Lozen on a beautiful mule for which her father had traded many pieces of turquoise. Lozen was dressed in a smock made of deerskin with a fringe around it which went down to her knees. She had a new pair of moccasins which came half way up her thighs. On the ride to the sacred mountain in the San Andreas Range she was reminded by her mother the chants she must use to honor Ussen. She schooled her in the way to construct the alter fire and explained that Ussen would come to her as she looked deeply and reverently into the hot coals while chanting the invocation that would open the doors to womanhood.

They left Ojos Caliente, rode down the box canyon of the Canada Alamosa and passed the Mexican village of Alamosa about noon. They stopped there briefly to visit with some of their friends and trade briefly before moving on. It was after dark when they reached the Rio Grande, having left the Canada Alamosa then veering south to the canyon of Cuchillo Negro, named for Lozen's Grandfather who had been Chief of the Warm Springs many years before.

They camped by the side of the Rio Grande waiting for the dawn and, when it came, they realized that the river had risen another foot that night and was in flood, ready to leave its banks. Lozen was terrified. She had never seen the water so high. But the family, after consulting, agreed that there was no choice but to cross. The consequences of not obeying the customs of initiation could be severe. After saying a prayer to the river God, Lozen's father cast pieces of turquoise into the roiling water and directed everyone else to do likewise.

The turquoise flashed in the early sun as they said their prayers and then, one by one, following Lozen's father, they plunged their mounts into the cold torrent. Lozen bent forward on her mule, her arms around his strong neck, urging him, "swim hard, swim fast." He was a very strong animal and Lozen was the first to reach the other bank, gratified that her mule had carried her up with such ease. All the riders made it across safely and they resumed their journey to the sacred mountain. They followed the trail up the great northern arm of Salinas Peak. All Warm Springs maidens and boys had followed the same trail from time immemorial to make their passages from childhood.

She was left alone in a cave on the eastern slope for four days and four nights without food to fast and pray before participating in the ceremony of womanhood. These four days and nights were a period of intense religious introspection for Lozen. She stared into the coals of her campfire which induced a trance revealing startlingly real visions. The visions revolved about her role as an Apache, her loyalty to her tribe, her duty to support her family, and her belief in Ussen, the creator of all, and finally culminated the last night in a surrealistic dream where Lozen saw herself suddenly divide and then divide again and continue to divide until she stood at the center of an expanding vision with transparent replicas of herself spreading further and further.

The further out the images went the fainter they became. The images multiplied and grew until suddenly there were so many that they faded into the distance. Then the whole vision collapsed and Lozen returned to consciousness.

When Lozen awoke she was sweating profusely. Already weakened from the fasting, she was beginning to hallucinate even while awake. Simply by closing her eyes the multiplying images would reappear to her. She would then banish the vision by opening her eyes then trying to understand its significance. She knew that Ussen was giving her some great power and that the secret of the power was contained within the vision. Finally, at midnight of the fourth day, she ceased to dream and drifted into a semi-comatose state and, breathing deeply, slept the rest of the night undisturbed.

When the escorting party came to retrieve Lozen, they found a changed person. The experience had strengthened her morally but had been a harrowing one both mentally and physically. On the way back to Ojos Caliente they again crossed the Rio Grande. The river was much lower. The prayers were made and the turquoise was tossed but there were no problems in making the other side nor the ten-hour trip back to Ojos Caliente. Lozen's family finished their packing chores and left to join the band. Lozen would undergo the four days of remaining ceremony deep in the Blue Mountains of Mexico.

The first night they camped at the southern tip of the Black Range and Lozen took the opportunity to confide in her mother the vision she had experienced during her ordeal on the mountain. She asked her mother's help in understanding what was the message that Ussen had given her. At the end of her account Lozen's mother looked at her daughter in disbelief and said, "Did you see this vision? Is this truly what occurred to you on the sacred mountain?"

Lozen answered, "Yes Mother, exactly. Every detail I have told you. What happened, did happen. I swear by Ussen. Have I ever lied you?"

Her mother responded, "No, you are a fine girl. I have not known you to lie, not one time. But," she said, "I have good reason to ask you some questions. What you have told me troubles me greatly."

Lozen was alarmed at her mother's obvious agitation and, tugging at her smock said, "Please mother, tell me, is there something bad about my dream? Is my power to die young? What is the meaning? Please mother, tell me."

"No daughter, there is no danger to you in your dream. I just want to be sure that this is not something that has happened to you because of what you have been told or heard. Do you understand?"

Lozen replied, "Yes Mother, I understand, but no one has ever told me I would have this dream."

Her mother pondered the answer and reflected before questioning Lozen further, "Daughter, have you ever heard anything about the powers of the great Chief Mahko?"

Lozen looked squarely at her mother and said, "No mother, I do not know what his powers were. I know that he was a great Chief, and that he was my father's ancestor, but I do not know about his powers. I have been told that he was a man of medicine as well as being Chief of all the Apache bands."

Lozen's mother said, "Yes, that is true, and I am also related to Mahko through my father, Cuchillo Negro, but I have never told you about the great powers of Mahko. I want to be sure that no one else has discussed these matters with you."

Lozen replied, "Mother, no one, not a whisper. I know nothing of the powers of Mahko."

The mother nodded her head up and down, and finally smiled and said, "Yes Daughter, I believe you. It's just that whenever I see a manifestation of the great Ussen I am overwhelmed and want to be sure that it is not an illusion or a mistake. I know now that what has happened to you has happened honestly, and not because of some story you've heard."

Lozen then pressed her mother to tell her more so finally she explained, "Daughter, one of the powerful images that Mahko saw when he underwent his four days of preparation for manhood was the dream of dividing and reproducing himself again and again, exactly as you have described, in circles growing ever larger and larger with the image growing fainter and fainter, and Tooklacan, a great medicine man, told Chief Mahko, 'You have star power, power to see what will happen in the future. While you are in one place, your mind will be in other places at the same time.'

"This is one of the greatest powers Ussen can give, because it protects the holder of the power and all those around him. You are very fortunate my daughter. Most of us have to anticipate danger by experience. I know you have heard the old saying that 'water is here, danger is near.' That is very true, but we must drink the water, so we must expose ourselves to danger. You have the power to know when the danger is real and not just a chance."

She continued, "We Apaches call this star power because the

stars are everywhere."

Then she added, "Daughter, at the same time I fear for you. For this power will set you aside and make you different from all other Apaches. If you were a man, it might make you a great Chief. But you are a woman and I fear that many of our people will misunderstand this great gift and ability to shield all the Apache people that Ussen has given you."

The following day, the family group left the Black Range. They followed the Mimbres River down to a point near Cook Springs where they turned abruptly to the west before striking south again for the Chiricahua Range. On the third day, they met the Bedonkohe band heading south and accompanied them on the rest of the journey. It was two days after the meeting of the bands that they reached the Chiricahua Mountains and spent two days with their close cousins, the Chiricahua Chokonen. Some of the Chokonen were to accompany them to the south while others stayed in their home range for the winter.

After resting with the Chiricahuas, the band of some four hundred men, women, and children moved south into the foothills of the Sierra Madre. Here they followed trails that led them deeper and deeper into the Blue Mountains of Mexico. Game was abundant everywhere. The Indians ate well and eagerly looked forward to the mild winter of the barrancas of the Blue Mountains.

Three days after penetrating the Blues they made contact with the Netdahe party which had been posted to escort them into the deeper canyons. They went down the Bavispe River and, in another three days, had reached a place called Santa Barbara where there were palm trees and fruit still in season. The air was balmy and filled with the fragrance of bougainvillea and other flowers. The young people were delighted and with their Netdahe cousins they busily engaged in bringing game back to the camp and exploring this wonderful subtropical land.

Lozen did not participate in these adventures but instead prepared for the important ceremony which would induct her into the role of a woman. Her mother and two aunts busily made the dress of pure white buckskin she would wear instead of the typical tan one. The ceremonial gown, when finished, was beaded and embellished with multiple layers of fringe and symbolic decorations.

Finally the day came when the assembled tribes met and the drums began to beat out the announcement that an Apache girl was to become an Apache woman. For four days and four nights the ceremonies continued and the bands celebrated with Lozen the center of all attention. She performed her tasks beautifully and, on the fourth day in front of everyone, she knelt and prayed and took her vows and became a woman. Lozen knew now she had to look forward to becoming a woman and a mother, carrying out her obligation to increase the population of the tribe. In her heart, she knew she was taking her vows with all the purpose and dedication any Apache maiden had ever taken upon the occasion but in a different way. She didn't know why, but she knew her task in life was not that of being a wife, that Ussen had set for her a course in life and a challenge that would be revealed when the time was right for her to know.

Lozen's mother and father and, indeed, all of her family, and for that matter, every Apache present, was proud of the way she held herself, her dignity, the fluid motion of her body as she performed the requisite dances. She was a jewel in the crown of the Apache tribe and a woman whom all expected would serve the Apache people well when called upon.

A month after the guests had arrived at Santa Barbara Canyon, Nantan Juh called a counsel of the Chiefs. They included Victorio and Nana of the Chihenne, and Loco of the Bedonkohe. All of the Indians assembled, some eight hundred strong, were invited to hear the parley. Juh announced that there were many young men in the group who had yet to serve as apprentices on a raid and that there were traditional enemies of the Apache, both to the east and to the west, who were encroaching upon the Apache domain.

Juh told the Chiefs assembled and the throng about them that, "The Tarahumara increase in numbers every year. They press in upon our hunting land and take up the river valleys to plant their corn and squash. Of late, they have even taken to raiding our rancherias and they must be taught a good lesson." He continued, "And to our west, the Mexicans push in closer, coming up the canyons, sending parties into the hills to prospect for the yellow metal and cut wood."

The Chiefs nodded their heads in agreement, appreciating full well the menace they faced on both sides because, to the north it was the same, only there it was the gringos and the Pueblo Indians.

Juh continued, "It is a good time for us to teach them a lesson with so many fine braves present and young men anxious to learn the ways of war. Let's strike first at the Tarahumaras and then at the Mexicans." Juh then called on Loco, Chief of the Bedonkohe, the band Juh had originally owed his own allegiance to as he had been born a Bedonkohe. He had become Chief of the mixed blood Netdahe only after marrying his first wife, a Netdahe.

Loco stood and agreed with Juh. "It is a good time for the young men to begin their apprenticeships and also important that the Apaches assert their southern boundary and join with their brothers, the Netdahe, in protecting the Apache strongholds."

Next, it was the turn of Victorio who stood and said, "I desire to hear from the oldest Chief among us, Nantan Nana, whose wisdom and advice I respect next to that of Ussen."

Nana arose, obviously in pain, his body racked with rheumatism and arthritis, and said, "Juh is the greatest war leader among us. His promise is known to all. It is an honor for every Apache to be here and join in the campaign with the Netdahe."

There were cries from the assembled throng, "It is true. It is true."

The war drum began to beat at the edge of the gathering. With the sounding of the drum, Victorio stood and said, "Chief Juh, we pledge ourselves to your leadership and join with you in defending the lands of the Apache."

With that, pandemonium broke loose and everyone rushed to the dance grounds knowing that there would be a party that would last all night long. A few jugs of aguamente and mescal that had been hidden in secret places, were brought out to entertain the guests and to celebrate the decision to punish the enemies.

All night the dance went on and many an eyebrow was raised when Lozen, unable to control herself, raced into the firelight and joined the young apprentice warriors who were dancing in celebration of their good fortune to go on a raid. Other young men who had had their baptism of fire, but needed to earn their spurs by participation in four campaigns, were eagerly celebrating this welcome opportunity to break from the doldrums of winter. The drums beat all night and the chants continued on and on and weary celebrants, one by one, finally dropped by the way until the dawn was breaking in the east and the last drum sounded its last throb. Only a few warriors were still dancing and a lone woman, Lozen.

The next several days, the large encampment made ready for their assault to the east against the Tarahumaras. The warriors were busy making arrows and extra bows while the women worked on preparing spare moccasin soles and sewing kits made from cactus spines and strong threads spun from the leaves. Extra water bottles were quickly woven and sealed with the pitch of the pine while meat was jerked into pemmican.

As these preparations went on, Lozen beseeched her brother and her father to permit her to go on the raid as an apprentice warrior. At first they paid no attention to her, dismissing her pleas almost with disdain. But Lozen continued to press her cause. Finally at the intercession of Nana, Lozen's father and brother agreed to bring it to the attention of Juh who, as resident Chief, was in charge of the expedition.

The three men and Lozen approached Juh's camp and told him what they wanted. Juh was amazed that any woman would even want to be involved with the business of war clearly the occupation of a man. Lozen was allowed to present her own case and she was very eloquent as she told Juh how strong she was, that there was no apprentice who could best her in any contest of skill or strength. Both her father and brother nodded their agreement at these assertions and Juh, looking at her athletic body and the muscles flexing under the tunic as she gestured energetically in her defense, could well believe that this was an exceptional woman when it came to strength and endurance.

It was, however, the comment of Nantan Nana that paved the way for Lozen's acceptance in the expedition. Nana brought out the point that a good tactician like Juh could appreciate.

He told him, "This is an unusual woman. When she went through her ordeal of maidenhood at our sacred mountain, she was visited by Ussen who gave her the same power that he gave Nantan Mahko, star power, the ability to foresee danger when it is at hand. She is more valuable to us than all of the spare ammunition we could carry. I ask, not for her, that she be permitted to join in this war against our enemy but I ask that all of us be given her protection so that we can campaign unafraid of ambush and surprise attack."

After Nana's comments, Victorio added his own assurance that Lozen had amazing powers. "This girl has clairvoyance; unbelievable clairvoyance. Time and time again, from her childhood, she has sensed when things were awry. I am her dedicated champion and do not approach you to quiet a vexing relative."

Convinced, Juh consented to Lozen accompanying the party. "Very well, but someone must claim her as an apprentice."

Nana promptly stood up and said, "I will claim that honor. I have no apprentice. As you all know, not many young men wish to follow me because of the demands I make upon them. I am without a young man to tend my horse and arms and provide me with assistance. I would like this Apache by my side."

Juh agreed that this was good. "There can be no better mentor for Lozen than the wise and respected Nana."

After a week of preparation the great war party of 250 braves and apprentices left the winter camp in Santa Barbara Canyon and spent three days working their way up the rocky gorge. Climbing out took almost an entire day, hauling themselves and their supporting supplies of ammunition and food to the mesa above. Then they headed east.

Half the warriors were mounted and the other half on foot.

Two more days were spent crossing canyons while moving to the east. Victorio explained to his sister that on a raid, to achieve surprise it was critical to come in from the direction that was the most difficult. For that reason, they had to avoid the canyon bottoms and move against the grain of the mountain chains.

They finally reached a precipice where they concealed themselves in a large depression. They could peer over the edge into the canyon below.

There were five rancherias in view with extensive fields of corn, squash, pumpkin, and beans being harvested by the busy Tarahumara. There appeared to be at least a thousand Indians in the rancherias. A formidable group to attack even with the Apaches large numbers. Juh called a conference of Chiefs and conferred along with some of the more notable warriors including Geronimo, a Bedonkohe. Though not a Chief himself, Geronimo was a medicine man and possessor of extraordinary powers including the power to find ammunition.

Juh gave an opinion to the others, "I think we should take the three middle camps. They are the ones that feel most secure and, undoubtedly, are the least defended. If we attack late in the afternoon, we can ransack those villages then leave and regain our position as dark falls. No doubt, there will be people who escape the onslaught and warn the other rancherias but they are going to be very timid about attacking a large group of Apaches until they know how many we are and where we are."

Everyone agreed to the plan and Nana volunteered to show the party down a trail he knew of that would take them from their camp to the bottom of the escarpment that night. He also knew of a large thicket at the bottom of the cliff where they could conceal themselves until the time came for their attack. Victorio and Loco agreed to the plan and the Chiefs disbanded and gave instructions to their various groups and, as night fell, everyone began the difficult descent down the escarpment. Apaches seldom moved at night in the summertime because of the danger of encountering snakes but the first frost had already come to the valley floor and it was thought that the rattlesnakes would be denned up away from the cold.

Lozen followed Nana who had the lead in going down the steep trail. Every once in a while Nana would stop and station a brave to guide those following. This was a precarious journey that few would attempt in the daylight. But the Apaches, in their desert mountain setting, were supreme in negotiating any terrain, at night or during the day, with safety and speed.

By dawn, all of the attacking party was assembled in the thicket. They spread out then rested, preparing for the battle that afternoon. The attacking force remained quiet throughout the day. The Chiefs conferred from time to time then passed instructions back to their men. When the sun was low in the west, Juh, who was to attack the middle camp with his Netdahe, gave the signal for the attack to begin with a blood curdling shout that was picked up by all the attackers who then rushed at the unsuspecting Tarahumara.

Nana advanced in front of the left flank attacking the northern most village with Lozen at his side holding his extra arrows and bows and eager for battle. She had no fear but, instead, was consumed with the passion of the battle taking place. She ran beside Nana flushed with excitement.

With the onslaught, the Tarahumara men did their best to defend their camps. Many of them did not have arms within reach so they ran because there was no hope in facing the fierce Apache warriors without any means of defense. There was a great flashing as lances, in the fading sunlight, flew through the air and caught the fleeing Tarahumaras in their backs while others were impaled in face-to-face combat. Some Tarahumaras had reached their weapons and were valiantly fighting back but within five minutes it was all over. The group led by Nana had not lost a brave but dozens of Tarahumara men lay dead and women and children huddled in their shelters pleading with the Apaches for mercy.

Nana and Victorio dispatched fifty warriors to harass the Tarahumara men who were fleeing while everyone else pitched in with the job of securing the spoils that were theirs. The young Tarahumara men and women capable of bearing burdens were quickly assembled and loaded down with skins and baskets filled with the harvest of corn, squash, pumpkins, and beans. All of the weapons that had been left behind were confiscated and wrapped up in hides and forced upon Tarahumara captives as burdens. The old women were left alone and, within an hour after the attack began, the Apaches had started back up the escarpment.

With an hour of daylight left, they were able to make the top, goading their captive burden-bearers with lances to hurry them on their way up. It was a tremendous tribute to the athletic ability of the Apaches and their captives that the entire force was able to evacuate the scene of battle and be back up to the camp by the time twilight was failing.

Fires were started and some preliminary celebrating began as they knew no one would follow them up that horrible trail at night. They could look over the rim and see the rancherias of the Tarahumaras down below, burning brightly, as they had all been torched before the retreat began. Juh directed everyone to rest for the night for early in the morning as first light appeared in the east, the entourage would start to retrace their steps.

The rear guard assignment was given to Nana who, next to Juh, was most familiar with the country they were passing through. By the end of the first day of retreat, they had crossed two of the intervening canyons and were only a day from the main camp when security relaxed a little and Nana permitted the rear guard to have a campfire. Still cautious, Nana had braves stationed an hour or two back on the trail to warn them of any who might be following with thoughts of reprisal.

That night he called Lozen to the fire and looked at her with a scowl and said, "You are my relative and I have sponsored you but you did not behave as an Apache apprentice. You were supposed to stand by me and replenish my arms. I saw you when two Tarahumaras confronted me take a lance and kill the one on the left. You did not have to do that. They were only armed with clubs and I could have disposed of both and besides, they were both in baby grass when I first killed an enemy of the Apache. But, my little sister, if I had truly been in danger, I would be grateful to you."

A smile then crept across the old weathered face and Lozen knew that the displeasure he voiced was only a mask to his gratitude and appreciation for her actions.

A day later, when they reached the main camp, it didn't take long for the warriors in Nana's party to spread the word that Lozen had killed a Tarahumara man. This was big medicine. There was much discussion. Some thought that Lozen should be punished for leaving her role as an apprentice and participating in the fight but others saw in Lozen a new Apache hero.

After the Tarahumara raid, all of the combatants rested and enjoyed the plaudits of their tribesmen. While they recuperated, Juh kept patrols constantly working to the east to be sure that there was no reprisal heading their way as they had captured many of the Tarahumara youth to indoctrinate as servants and later to become wives and warriors. At the same time, Juh sent three scouting groups to the west to determine whether or not there were any Mexican troops in the Sonoran plains bordering on the Sierra Madre.

A month after the strike against the Tarahumaras, Juh called a counsel of the Chiefs and proposed that they wage a three-pronged offensive into Sonora. The purpose was to discourage the Mexicans from settling in the fertile canyons and valleys of the Sierra Madre and to capture horses, mules, and other supplies needed to survive the winter.

Nana observed, "It's high time we paid a visit to our Mexican 'friends' and let them know we haven't forgotten their treacheries."

Geronimo, who had been asked to sit with the Chiefs because of his great knowledge and influence, eagerly embraced Nana's remarks. After all, he had lost a wife and three children to Mexican guile in the town of Janos. There was agreement that the campaign should be launched at once.

When word spread through the bands, excitement ran high. The young warriors from the North were all champing at the bit, having been held in abeyance by the Chiefs in order not to antagonize the white-eyes. Here in Mexico it was different. The rules of warfare were what they had been for centuries. To the victor went the spoils.

Juh and the Netdahe, reinforced with Chiricahua, were to take the middle and attack the Mexican village of Cucurpe. Victorio and Nana were to take the left flank and scour the countryside for horses and targets of opportunity. Chief Loco and the Bedonkohe were to do the same on the right flank.

The task force pulled out of the winter camp of Santa Barbara with close to three hundred warriors and novices enrolled. It was the largest war party that had ever been organized to attack the Mexicans in Sonora. For a day they rode down the Santa Barbara Canyon and then started across the ridges leading to the plains where the villages and haciendas were located.

Before they left the cover of the mountains, a final council of war was held and the places for rendezvous selected. Offerings were made to Ussen to ensure the success of the mission.

Lozen's spectacular performance against the Tarahumaras had assured her a place beside Nana once again. No one criticized her inclusion in the war party after her success as an apprentice in the attack on the Tarahumaras. As they rode down the canyon, Victorio, Lozen, and Nana were abreast and in front of the Warm Springs band which was bringing up the rear guard. Victorio looked at his two companions in wonderment. Here was an old man who had already lived a lifetime and still was one of the most feared and capable warriors in all the Apache bands and alongside him rode his own sister; different from any other woman he had ever known. Handsome and attractive and yet hardly a suitable mate because she excelled in everything that she did and put most of the men in the band to shame. Victorio himself had felt feelings of jealousy towards her. Why should any woman be able to compete with him and yet, throughout his life, his sister had been a threat time and time again.

Geronimo, two days earlier, had expressed some interest in Lozen and wondered if she might want to be his third wife although he hastily added, "But if she has no interest, please do not press her.

I am very happy with my families as they are."

Victorio acknowledged his disclaimer of ardor with a wry smile. "I understand Uncle. You are like everyone else and it is a wise Apache who knows when to fight and when to run."

Well, so be it, thought Victorio as they moved along down the canyon, *if Lozen wants to fight, let her fight. She will be shown no favoritism, given no special treatment. She is on her own the same as any man and her performance will acquit or condemn her.*

When the Chihenne reached the point where they left the Santa Barbara Canyon and started cross-country, the going got really rough. Three days later they reached the Sonoran Plains, having lost only three horses but no Apaches. It was here that Juh had waited for the column to close and they held their final counsel of war. Early the next morning the Apaches struck out on their missions. As soon as Juh's Netdahes had moved out, Victorio gave the signal, by raising his arm and extending it towards his left, for the Chihenne to start their advance. He had divided his command of almost a hundred warriors into five groups with Nana and Lozen on the far left. He realized this might be the most dangerous place but was determined that Lozen prove herself.

The first few miles were uneventful. They passed several ranches with cattle and horses grazing in fields but they pressed on hoping to find larger and better herds to attack. By midmorning, they were well out of the plains and were encountering larger haciendas.

There was considerable distress on the part of the local inhabitants with this large number of Apaches flooding through the country. Runners had been dispatched to the various towns to warn them that attack might be imminent. Victorio's groups, however, were bypassing the towns and leaving them alone. When they came upon larger herds of horses and mules they swept down and quickly cut out the animals they wanted and by noon had started back towards the first rendezvous with more than 300 animals. Lozen was exhilarated. This was where she belonged. This was being alive and she pressed keenly on the heels of the animals she was driving back toward the first rendezvous point.

From the clouds of dust at their rear, it was obvious they were being followed but at a respectable distance. Clouds of dust were rising elsewhere on the plains as other Apache groups were accomplishing their missions. While every Mexican in Sonora might be in back of them, no one felt that they posed any danger. Lozen rode up alongside Nana to be sure she discharged her duty as his apprentice.

As she reigned in beside him Nana smiled, saying, "Well, little sister, you finally remembered that you are responsible to me. I wondered if I was to be without an apprentice on this mission."

Lozen was at first chagrined and then smiled broadly realizing that Nana was teasing her. With tongue in cheek she replied, "Great Nantan Nana, if you had a hundred apprentices, they would not be visible in your presence."

Nana reached over, gently patted her hand, and said, "I will not argue the point. It is enough that you are with me."

Lozen reigned tightly on her horse, bringing it to a stop, leaving Nana to surge ahead. Then, raking her mount on the withers, she sprang forward, catching up with Nana and grabbing the reigns of his horse and bringing it to a halt. "Nana," she called, "I have a feeling that we are in great danger. Something is amiss. Something has gone wrong. I do not know what it is but we may be in trouble."

Nana knew that this girl had amazing powers and could see things that no one else could. He called out to the braves of the group to close up the gaps then they cautiously approached the next ridge.

As they topped the ridge, they saw before them a squadron of Mexican soldiers. Not rurales or townspeople, but hardened veterans of the regular army. They were formed on the plain in line, two abreast, and a hundred strong. Just then, Victorio, with another twenty braves appeared on their left and shouted orders to drive the captured remuda straight for the middle of the Mexican Cavalry. By hand signals, the command passed to all of the warriors and everyone piled in, shouting as they jostled the stock forward. With the added animals being driven by Victorio, the din of the hoofbeats sounded like thunder in the skies and the Mexican veterans began to appreciate that their trap might well become a graveyard for themselves.

As the first of the animals reached the Mexican lines, the soldiers gave way and, wheeling rapidly, sought to retreat and avoid the stampede. When this happened, the outer flanks, fearing that they were left alone to withstand the Apaches, bolted to the right and left. As a result, the Mexican force was split into three groups and the Apaches rapidly pushed against the middle, driving the stock ahead, content to watch the Mexican soldiers flee, no longer a cohesive force.

Throughout, Lozen rode close to the side of Nana, ready to carry out her duties as an apprentice. It was one of the easiest battles the Apaches had ever fought. Not one arrow had been loosed. Not one gun fired. Not a lance had sought a target. The stolen animals they drove before them had carried the day. And when late that afternoon they reached the first rendezvous, they were all bubbling with stories of their bloodless conquest of the Mexican army.

By nightfall, all of the strike forces had returned to the rendezvous point and everyone eagerly told the stories of their victories. The Bedonkohe, to the right, had been as successful as the Chihenne in gathering horses and mules while Juh and his Netdahe and Chiricahua had sacked the Mexican town of Cucurpe, carrying off many captives, horses and beeves, and a half dozen mules loaded with aguamente and mescal.

Three days later, when the war party reached the winter camp, the celebrating was without equal. There had never been a raid with such achievement. At that moment, when everyone felt that there was nothing that could be said or done to eclipse their success, Geronimo, who had failed to make the first rendezvous, came in with, to no one's great surprise, a complete pack train of ammunition and military supplies. If there was an Apache who did not believe Geronimo had the power to find ammunition, after that day, he held his counsel.

The celebration went on for three days and the only Apaches

who didn't join the drunken orgy were Nana, Lozen, and Nana's small band, all of whom were sworn to abstain from alcohol; plus those who were on duty guarding the rear to be sure the Mexicans didn't follow them in from the plains. There was no chance of that. The news of the extensive raid spread throughout Sonora. Never had the Apaches struck in such force and there was no one among the Mexican military or the townspeople who wished to press their luck tackling the Apaches on their home ground.

At the height of the celebration, Geronimo and Juh, both inebriated, announced to the throng that they had concluded a pact calling for the marriage of Ishtee, the sister of Geronimo, to Juh, the Chief of the Netdahe.

The wedding proceeded immediately and for four more days the festivites continued as the wedding ceremony was celebrated. On the forth night of the marriage revelry, Lozen and Nana were tending a small fire on the outskirts of the camp, avoiding the abandon of their tribal kin in the jubilation of all of the wonderful things that had occurred.

Nana looked at Lozen and said, "Little sister, remember this night. It might be the last moment of joy our people ever have."

Lozen nodded her assent, adding, "Yes, Nantan, it is unlikely that we'll ever again be so successful as a people. Perhaps Ussen has given us this moment of joy to compensate for what lies ahead."

"It is true," added Nana. "It is true," he repeated. "The future is filled with fighting and bloodshed. It is only a matter of time before the white-eyes press in on us and take our homeland away."

Lozen's vivid and abundant dreams of those wonderful days of Apache freedom slowly faded into a deep and restful sleep.

CHAPTER THREE

Capture

Three weeks after the Tres Castillos disaster, forty warriors and their families were assembled together. Some remained in isolated hideouts while a large group of the Netdahe and some Chihenne, responding to pressure from the U.S. Army, had moved onto the reservation at San Carlos. With the group assembled, Nana planned a series of raids up and down the Black Range, striking at Hillsboro, the Rio Grande Valley, and as far as Magdelena and Silver City. The purpose of the raids, in addition to revenge for the death of Victorio, was to capture horses, pack animals, rifles, and ammunition.

The Army poured reinforcements into the Black Range; reacting to scouting reports that activity had shifted to this wild, inaccessible country. The Apaches watched the soldiers go up and down the valleys. They knew exactly where they were every minute of the day and permitted them to approach their camps and hideouts only to fade away when attack was imminent. Many a small detachment was wiped out in ambush after ambush as the Apaches led the soldiers on and then picked them off at will from the ridgelines where they lay in wait. Very few Apaches were lost but they were constantly harried and forced to move with all semblance of normal tribal life having ceased. They were waging war twenty-four hours a day, their only reserves being guts and determination.

Throughout this ordeal, Lozen stayed at the side of Nana who cleared all of his plans with her and constantly sought her visionary powers to protect his excursions. When called on to serve her people, Lozen would close her eyes and chant a special prayer to Ussen and then relay her visions of the nearness of danger. On some occasions, after Lozen had warned Nana not to attempt a raid or strike, scouts reported that the American troops had been lying in wait and were nearby and capable of delivering a serious blow to the Apaches. As a result, Lozen's reputation as a medicine woman grew daily.

No one could believe that Nana was still alive. He would not tell his age but it was obvious he was an old man. He was crippled with arthritis and in constant pain but he could still ride a horse to its death and he personally led every major raid. His amazing vigor and passion to extract vengeance for the Tres Castillos massacre gave the others strength and will to carry on.

Lozen rode alongside Nana and became his trusted lieutenant, every bit a warrior. Everyone agreed that had Lozen been a man she would easily have been elected to succeed Victorio as Chief of the Chihennes. This was not to take away from Nana who could have been the principal Chief many years earlier. Nana, however, was more than content to work under the direction of Victorio. Nana was an outstanding tactician and fearless warrior but he preferred not to be involved with the politics of leadership, leaving that to others so he could concentrate on the areas where he was best endowed.

At this time, a new and alarming development took place in the campaign of the white-eyes against the Warm Springs Apaches, involving the use of Indian scouts. Since the very beginning of the Warm Springs uprising, the Army had used Pueblo scouts from the Ysleta del Sur Pueblo in El Paso, Texas and they had acquitted themselves with distinction but now they had discovered that there was an even more potent weapon to use against the Apaches and that was the Apache himself.

They started by using Tonto and Ben-et-dinne Apaches from San Carlos as scouts and, before the campaign was over, they turned the Warm Springs against themselves.

The Pueblos were brave and effective warriors. They entered into the scouting assignment as soldiers of the U.S. Army with pleasure for they were traditional enemies of the Apaches. They had not, however, been raised as Apaches and did not understand the Apache thinking and methods of warfare as well as the Apaches themselves.

These Apache scouts also introduced a completely new element into the pattern of guerilla warfare which Nana carried out. This was the ability of the scouts to track the retreating Warm Springs at close range on foot. The mountain ranges could not be utilized effectively by horses. The cavalry, when they got near to an Apache group, had to dismount in order to engage them. This immediately gave the Apaches an advantage as their physical condition and ability to negotiate the rough country was far superior to the American troops. That was not the case with respect to the Apache scouts who were able to put much greater pressure on Nana and his forces.

Nana, with the band assembled at Frank's Mountain, stated, "I believe the time has come when we must leave our home land. If we stay here any longer we will be defeated. With the Apache scouts helping the white-eyes it is only a matter of time before their numbers will make it impossible for us to move from one place to another. I think we must move to the Blue Mountains of Mexico where we will be able to heal our wounds and enjoy our families and survive with our hearts and heads held high."

All of the warriors agreed that this was best and the decision was approved heartily by the women who, constantly on the run, were unable to tan hides or make moccasins or do any of the other tasks that were necessary to maintain family integrity.

Nana sent the women and children under Lozen to work their way southward along the spine of the Black Range until they reached the rendezvous point east of Santa Rita. No warriors accompanied this group as every man was going to be needed to provide a covering feint to the northeast. The twenty-eight warriors fit for combat were divided into three groups and a series of raids were instituted for a week that caused the middle Rio Grande to fear that once again Europeans were going to be ejected from New Mexico as they had been during the Pueblo revolt of 1680.

No town was safe with the exception of Alamosa. It was spared because of the fair and honorable dealings the Warm Springs had always received from their Spanish and Mexican friends. No one else was excepted and the cavalry was frantically wiring for reinforcements and concentrating every available man at the north end of the Black Range and throughout the San Mateos and the North Gila. On the seventh day, the warriors all hastily beat a retreat to the south and joined forces with Lozen and the woman and children at the rendezvous near Santa Rita. Here the Apache force, with everyone mounted, struck out on an evening march across the desert, reaching a secluded canyon near Stein's Pass by morning. It was unusual for the Apaches to make nighttime marches as they felt uncomfortable and, in particular, were concerned about encountering rattlesnakes. Rattlesnakes were one of the few things that the Apaches feared, preferring to face the grizzly or the mountain lion with a knife in hand, rather than risk being bitten by the master of the desert nights.

They spent the day holed up in a box canyon with lookouts posted at every vantage point. The lookouts spotted a column of cavalry on the road from Lordsburg to Deming accompanied by a force of several Apache scouts. While the group passed within four miles of the main forces of Nana, they were unaware of their presence. But Nana knew that they would cut their trail if they turned north towards Silver City as he expected them to. This would mean immediate pursuit. They pushed on as soon as it was dusk, crossing the Lordsburg road and heading towards the western end of the Dragoons where they could find sanctuary in the foothills of the Sierra Madre across the border before the break of dawn.

The group pressed hard throughout the night and, although individuals were separated from each other at times, they managed to meet as dawn was breaking at the rendezvous point, a cool spring on the flank of the Sierra Madre foothills. Here they rested while lookouts were posted on the heights above. The sun had only been in the sky for a few hours when the lookouts reported back that there was a large cloud of dust to the north and that its size meant that it was a much larger force than the detachment they had seen the day before.

Nana called for a counsel of all the warriors and asked Lozen if she could use her powers to tell if this was the only force against them. Lozen chanted a prayer to Ussen and pressed her hands to her temples and sought to be one with the environment, hoping that a premonition would guide her advice to Nana. After several seconds she opened her eyes and told the Chief that all she could feel was foreboding and danger in every direction. This was depressing news because, until they reached the Sierra Madre, they were particularly vulnerable to pursuit by cavalry. The Apaches' mounts were completely jaded from two nights of forced marching, and they had no remuda to call upon.

Nana divided his forces to prevent the women and children from being an impediment to rapid retreat if they were discovered. He had Lozen gather the women and children and the supply animals and start off immediately, skirting the mountain that they were camped under, in order to strike an old Apache trail leading to the Blue Mountains. He sent five warriors to act as guard for this force and deployed his remaining men in an ambush to delay the advance of the pursuing Mexicans so that the women and children could escape to the security of the Netdahe stronghold. Nana's plan was one that had worked time after time and it would have given the Apaches an excellent opportunity of escape without losses had it not been for a second force of Mexican cavalry which was coming up from the Southwest in response to frantic warnings being telegraphed all the way along the border that Nana had left the Black Range and was heading into Old Mexico to join up with Juh and Geronimo.

The Apaches had just started up the trail on the side of the mountain when they ran into the Mexican forces coming down the trail in the opposite direction. They had reached a small draw making a steep descent from the mountain when they saw the front ranks of the cavalry coming towards them scarcely a hundred yards away. The Mexican advance riders saw the Apaches at the same instant and let out a cry of warning to their fellow soldiers. This was a group of irregulars that had been raised from various towns in Chihuahua. They deployed in combat formation and charged the Indians.

As the Mexican cavalry began its charge, Lozen and the five braves dismounted and, using the bank of the arroyo as a breastwork, launched a withering and accurate fire into the advancing line of cavalry. At the first sight of the Mexican force, Lozen had sent a young woman noted for her running ability to the rear to advise Nana that they were under attack.

After the first repulse, the Major in charge of the militia called out to his men, "Dismount and form a skirmish line." The horses were taken to the rear and the rurales were ordered to work their way forward on their bellies to engage the Apaches hand-to-hand.

The Mexican commander had no idea that the force he was opposing consisted almost entirely of women and children. In the excitement of the encounter, no effort had been made to determine how many warriors they were facing. The withering fire put up by Lozen and the five warriors had convinced the Mexicans to a man that they were up against the entire Apache Nation. If at this moment the bugler had sounded retreat, he would have been trampled by the irregulars eagerly obeying his command before the last note sounded.

For two hours, the Mexicans cautiously advanced as the Apaches waited patiently and, from time to time picked off one of the soldiers when he exposed himself. If the Major had flanked either up or down the canyon in an envelopment, he would have had the Apaches at his mercy since his force of forty men outnumbered the Apaches with weapons seven to one.

As the fight progressed, Lozen moved from warrior to warrior, giving them words of encouragement telling them, "The main force will be here soon to help you. Make every shot count." She also checked on ammunition and made sure that the women and children remained huddled under the bank, protected from enemy fire. The men readily accepted Lozen's assumption of command and afterwards, around Apache campfires, the story was told of the woman Nantan who had saved the women and supplies from certain annihilation with great judgment and fighting spirit.

Three hours after the battle had commenced, the main Apache fighting force made its appearance. The troops engaging Lozen's little group almost gave up the field upon seeing so many reinforcements pouring into the small canyon. But then they heard the shots and cries of the Mexican regulars who were hot on the trail of Nana and his fighters. Nana conferred with Lozen who told him her estimate of the number of Mexicans in front of them and commented that it would be impossible to escape down the canyon as that led to the floor of the Chihuahuan desert.

Lozen told Nana, "As soon as it is dark, we should retreat up the canyon if the Mexicans have not cut us off."

Nana agreed and positioned his men to harass the Mexicans on both sides. They were in a tight spot but one thing in their advantage was that the bullets of one group of Mexicans that overshot their mark were raising hell with the group on the other side. The estimate of the Apaches facing them miraculously rose even higher.

After Nana arrived, he sent four warriors to climb up the canyon and find secure positions as high up as they could to torment the Mexicans and discourage their enveloping the Apache position from that side. This maneuver saved the day as the Lt. Colonel in command of the Mexican regulars, noting the fire from above, attempted to make contact with the other force by sending a lieutenant and squad of men below the canyon. After the lieutenant returned and advised him of the number of troops and the status of their ammunition supply, he took a third of his men and directed them to take positions down the canyon and began working their way up.

He knew that he was facing about twenty warriors and he had

fifty men with him. He didn't know, however, how many Apache warriors were in the other band with which they had joined forces. The Major had estimated them to be at least fifty. The commander, as a result, was very cautious in planning his advance and lost the advantage of daylight.

The Apaches were putting up a good account for themselves and even though the circle of attackers closed ever inward, they were taking ground at a high price. An hour before dark, Nana became aware that all of the warriors were running short of ammunition and some were down to their last two or three bullets. He passed the word to make every shot count.

Nana asked Lozen, "Quick, Lozen, where is the reserve ammunition? We're running low."

Lozen replied, "The mule carrying the ammunition was hit when we first encountered the Mexicans. It is about forty feet in front of us in that direction." She pointed directly at the besieging Mexicans.

Nana surveyed the situation and said, "I will find someone to attempt to retrieve the ammunition."

The first warrior sent out was killed before he reached the dead mule. The second got to the mule and loosened a bag of ammunition and began dragging it back towards the Apache lines when he was also struck by a bullet and wounded so badly he could not carry on.

Lozen, without waiting for Nana to send another warrior to his death, boosted herself over the arroyo embankment and raced to the side of the wounded warrior. On reaching her fallen comrade, she slipped the strap of the ammunition bag over her shoulder and then, grasping hold of him with her left arm, began pulling him towards the arroyo embankment. A bullet had broken the femur of his right leg and he had great difficulty helping her. The pain was intense as he struggled with injured legs and arms to make ground towards safety.

When they were ten feet from the embankment, the warrior was hit again by a rifle bullet. This time it was in the head and he was killed instantly. They were in an opening in the brush which offered no cover and, realizing that she might suffer the same fate at any minute, Lozen stood up and swung the ammunition bag around her head one time and sent it flying into the arroyo before she flattened herself to the ground again.

Lozen's action drew a withering fire from both Mexican forces which could see her clearly when she stood up and tossed the bag. Years later, speakers who recounted the bravery of Lozen this day would swear, "A hundred Mexican bullets passed through the air searching for her body without success. Her powers must have stopped the bullets in flight."

The sun was now low on the horizon and Nana, replenished with ammunition, passed the word to all the Apaches to commence a withering fire and, on his signal, to head up the arroyo, every man for himself, and meet at the rendezvous previously pointed out. As the last light was fading, the Mexican troops, having enveloped the Apaches on three sides, began a final charge in order to deny the Apaches the screen of darkness and possible escape. As the attack began, Nana gave the alarm and every warrior discharged his rifle at the onrushing Mexicans and immediately broke up the canyon. It was impossible to save all, but the darkness did permit three-fourths of the Apaches to make good their escape. In the nighttime there was no way the Mexican troops could hunt them down.

Lozen ran straight up the canyon hoping to draw the attention of the Mexicans. She was a fast runner and felt that she could assist the women and their children by being a target. Her strategy worked and the first of the soldiers pounding on horseback up the canyon took her trail, passing a dozen or more women and children who had huddled along the bank in pockets of brush from which they subsequently were able to escape.

As the horsemen neared Lozen, she turned and dodged the lance of the first soldier, but the barrel of the carbine of the second crashed into her right temple and knocked her unconscious to the ground.

As soon as the battle was concluded, the Mexican Colonel assessed his casualties and examined the prisoners, finding that there were ten Apache women and fifteen youngsters securely tied by thongs and under guard of the Mexican irregulars. Quickly he decided that he would leave the prisoners in their care and ordered them transported to Janos while he took the regular forces under his command and attempted a circuit of the mountain by night, hoping to be in a position to intercept the Apaches when they descended on the other side.

The Mexicans finished their dinner and when it was over, gathered around the blazing campfire, congratulating themselves on their victory. Their exultation was considerably reinforced with copious amounts of mescal which they had pulled from their saddlebags. The Major made no effort to maintain discipline as he was a townsman himself and could not afford to invoke the displeasure of his peers. Within an hour, they were so worked up and intoxicated that it was readily agreed that they should enjoy the fruits of their victory.

One of them, swaggering around the fire, proclaimed to the others, "Let's teach these Apache whores that they can do better making love to a man than fighting him."

A shout of agreement went up and immediately everyone looked at the women in order to pick out the one that would be his. One man went over to an Apache girl of thirteen who had yet to undergo initiation into womanhood and proclaimed, "This one is for me. I killed the most Apaches so I get to have first choice."

A howl of protest went up.

One soldier cried, "Oh no you didn't. That honor is mine. I should be given first choice." Several others joined in and proclaimed that they had earned the designation and privilege.

Another shouted, "Let's play cards. I have a deck. We all fought bravely today and lady luck can decide who has the first choice."

One group of soldiers played a game of Monte and determined a winner. A second group took on the challenge of the card game as the first group went to the Apache women and untied the young girl who was thrown on the ground with a man on each side, holding down her arms and legs while the winner tore off her tunic, exposing her bare flesh to the glare of the fire.

The winner, with the help from the other men, spread the young girl's legs apart and, having dropped his pants, penetrated her with a savage lunge. The young girl screamed and attempted to flail at her captors, all to no avail as the man continued to ravage her, finally standing over her after he had had his way. By this time, the young girl was in a state of hysteria and was sobbing in great spasms. The other women were shocked and felt so much pity for the poor young girl that they failed to appreciate their own danger. The children stared in horror, not knowing what was really happening, but gaining a hatred of white-eyes that would never die or even abate.

The second game of Monte concluded and another victim was selected with the same result as the first. This time the woman was older and put up a better fight but the horror and shock to the Apache captives was the same. When the second woman was raped, the soldiers, not wanting to wait for their turn at the Monte game, followed one at a time until a dozen men raped her.

The third game of Monte produced a winner who was the town bully, a huge man, well over six feet tall and weighing in excess of 200 pounds and known for his brute strength and "machismo".

He walked to where the women were tied and stopped in front of Lozen saying, "This one is long in years but I think maybe she has what it takes to make a man satisfied. Cut her loose and we'll find out."

It took four men to throw Lozen down after she was untied, and when they ripped her clothing off they knew they were not dealing with a thirteen-year old girl. Here was a woman who was muscled like a man. The braggart dropped his trousers and knelt to the ground and placing his hands inside the knees of Lozen, began to force her legs apart. That began a battle that nearly rivaled the day-long battle in the canyon as Lozen fought like a cornered tiger, breaking a hand loose and scratching, biting anything that came near her mouth, kicking with her feet. One blow of her right foot landed directly on the groin of the would be rapist. The man on the right hand side who was holding her left arm made the mistake of attempting to push back the head of Lozen and she clamped down with her strong teeth and bit into his hand. Her teeth reached the bone, almost severing the first finger. The soldier screamed loudly and, picking up a rock, smashed it into the left side of Lozen's head. The blow was a glancing one, crossing the side of Lozen's face and opening up a great gash along her forehead. Blood spouted profusely as Lozen struggled, splattering all of the men engaged in the assault.

Suddenly the bully stood up, pulled up his trousers and said, "Not this one. God help the man who is married to her, surely she will kill him."

The rest of the attackers withdrew a few feet and looked at Lozen lying there, her body heaving as the blood pulsed from the wound. At this turn of events the Major regained his sanity and ordered that two of the Apache women be released to tend to Lozen and the other women who had been violated.

The ardor of the troops cooled dramatically and the rest of the women were spared the ordeal of the first three. As the women attended to Lozen, wiping her forehead and staunching the blood by putting a compress, made by splitting the leaf of a Nopal plant, on her face and forehead they told Lozen that her power had saved her. One exclaimed, "It is truly a miracle. Ussen himself has forbidden your rape."

After the three women had been treated by their colleagues, they were tied up again and kept under guard for the rest of the night. In the morning they were forced to march thirty-five miles to the village of Janos where they were placed in the town jail. The men of this expedition told everyone in town that one of the Apache prisoners was a tiger but they did not recount what had actually happened that night. With the effects of the liquor gone, they were ashamed and dismayed by their conduct.

After two days, the women and children were transferred by ox cart to the town of Chihuahua, a three-day trip. There they were kept under lock and key for a week while arrangements were made to transport them to Mexico City. The Mexican authorities knew that unless the Apaches were sent to the other side of the country, they would do nothing but think out a plan of escape and make their way back to their tribe. By the time they reached Chihuahua, Lozen's wound, which had not been stitched, became badly infected and a doctor was called in to lance a large abscess and administer stitches. He told the corporal assisting him that he had never seen a patient so insensitive to pain as Lozen, not knowing that she felt every bit of the torture that he inflicted, but that she stoically refused to indicate the least sign of its effect.

Apache Tears

CHAPTER FOUR

Escape

Two weeks later, the captives were loaded onto four carretillas after preparations were completed to begin the journey to Mexico City. Twice a day, the carretillas would stop and the women and children were permitted to relieve themselves but always under the watchful eye of the half-dozen soldiers who were along as guards. Lozen waited until the fourth day, the Apache sacred number, and when they were making one of the stops to permit relief, she managed to pick up a jagged piece of flint without being noticed by the guards. She kept the stone concealed in the fold of her moccasin until that night. After dinner, their captors confined them to the carretillas and secured them with additional leather strips. Stealthily, and again without being noticed, she retrieved the flint and cut through her bindings.

In the carretilla with Lozen were two other women without children and another woman with three children, the youngest of which was only a year old. They conferred in low whispers and decided that the woman with the children had to stay behind with the youngest child as it might give them away as they slipped through the night.

This woman, who was also a niece of Lozen, readily agreed. It was the Apache custom to sacrifice for the interest of the tribe. With that decided, the three women and the two older children slowly lowered themselves from the carretilla and slipped through the dimly lit campground unnoticed by the sentinel who, fortunately, had his back turned to them and was dozing.

Earlier, Lozen had carefully sized up the country as they made their stop for the day. When they were far enough from the campsite to make there escape a reality, she immediately led them to an outcropping of rocks lying to the east with her fellow Apaches following in single file closely behind her. They traveled all night and by dawn were fifteen miles from where they had made their escape.

Lozen was sure they would not be followed as the guards would have their hands full escorting the other prisoners to Santa Barbara, the next stop, where no doubt they would alert the army to come in pursuit of the women and children. When it became light, the little group stopped under a bluff in a dry wash and slept for four hours. Lozen awakened them saying, "We must go on."

She cautioned them, "Be extremely careful with your moccasins, as we have no leather with which to attach as new soles." While they could improvise needles and thread from the cactus, they would have to scavenge their own wearing apparel for sole leather.

They covered another thirty miles by dark. As they entered the foothills of the Sierra Madre, the cover became much better. They had gone a day and a night without food, except for some cactus leaves they had skinned and munched to sustain their strength and abate their thirst. They camped alongside a large oak tree which had recently fallen. The next morning Lozen busied everyone preparing slings from their clothing so they could attempt to catch rabbits. Lozen, herself, prepared several snares and by noon they had three jackrabbits roasting on a fire.

They did not cook the rabbits on spits. They were gutted and placed directly on the coals and turned once after the down side had been thoroughly blackened. The carcasses were then opened and the succulent meat removed from the charred skin and devoured instantly by the starving Apaches.

Lozen's wound was infected again and the women split some nopal cactus leaves to act as a compress and dressing. The small group rested for a couple of hours and then set out again heading northwest, starting towards the brooding peaks of the Blue Mountains of the Sierra Madre. Lozen had never been on this flank of the range before but she had, since she was a little girl, sat around the fires listening to the tales of the braves as they described their adventures throughout the southwest and was quite confident that she was heading for Juh's stronghold.

The next day they caught two more rabbits and lucked upon a wild turkey with a large brood of half-grown poults. They gleefully chased down four and that evening enjoyed a banquet. They were now in the pinewood forest and gaining altitude rapidly. They reached the top of a rounded mountain which was almost flat in places. They walked rapidly for several miles until they came to a cliff which dropped vertically to the canyon below with a mountain stream running through it.

One of the children excitedly pointed up stream and said, "Rancheria! Rancheria!" They looked up the river course and there along its sides were several jacales. There was also smoke coming from the general area. Lozen told them all to drop to the ground. This was not an Apache rancheria. It was either a village of the white-eyes or the Tarahumaras, the white-eyes' allies. It certainly must be avoided. Lozen realized that it would be utterly impossible to descend the cliff at night as it was almost sheer and that they would have to work their way through the crevices; that every foot and handhold would be precarious for a successful descent. A nighttime traverse would be out of the question.

Reluctantly, they detoured along the canyon precipice for two miles before daring to negotiate a passage down the cliff. They descended to a large tributary canyon which provided them with a fairly easy path down to the ravine below. By the time they reached the bottom, the meat they had saved from their successful turkey hunt was gone and they were very hungry. They had not dared to light a fire with the danger of enemies so close at hand. When they crossed the swiftly flowing mountain stream, they could see that it was generously supplied with fish but even their hunger could not break the taboo of the Apaches to avoid animals that lived in the water.

After crossing the stream, they reconnoitered the cliffs in front of them. Lozen went upstream and the other women went the other direction while the children waited. Downstream they found a side canyon almost as broad as the canyon they were in and Lozen decided that would be the one they would use to reach the top of the other side.

They dropped down the main canyon a mile to where the side canyon entered and turned up it following the course of a small stream. By late afternoon, Lozen felt they were safe and allowed the group to build a fire using fire sticks they had made. They felt secure because of Lozen's power of knowing when there was danger and she was obviously relaxed at the time. They quickly fanned out in groups and hunted for rabbits and birds while Lozen set snares. By nightfall, they had plenty of rabbits and small birds to satisfy their hunger and replenish the larder for the trip ahead.

The next day they reached the top of another mountain and continued northwesterly for four hours at which time they came to the walls of a canyon. Looking across, Lozen knew they had reached the stronghold of Juh which was a broad mountaintop, heavily forested and filled with game and fresh water. It was accessible from the north where a zigzag trail reached the flat top of the mountain itself. Unfortunately, they were on the wrong side of the mountain and they had to drop down a steep side canyon and circle for another day before they could reach the trail they needed to begin their journey up.

As they climbed, Lozen cautioned her charges to be careful where they stepped. If they slipped from the trail, there was no chance of survival. When they neared the rim of the mountain, they saw an Apache warrior on a rock watching them. He motioned with his hand to come on and they did, recognizing their good friend Laughing Boy.

He was happy to see Lozen and her friends one of which was his own mother. He escorted them to the camp where Nana, Geronimo, and Juh were waiting for word of the survivors of the attack in the canyon. They had given up hope that any more would come in. They gathered about Lozen and the other survivors as they listened to their story and were saddened to find that many of their friends and relatives were bound by carretilla to slavery in Mexico City.

That night a celebration was held for Lozen and her fellow escapees. Before Juh gave the signal for the drums to start beating, he respectfully asked Lozen if there was danger near. She kneeled and sought the guidance of Ussen as she had so many times in the past. Rising from her meditation she told the relieved throng, "No, there is no danger near." It was almost dawn before the great drum quit pounding across the canyon.

Lozen slept late the next day. When she awoke, she visited with Nana to determine what had happened after the battle of the canyon. Nana told her that only five Apaches were unaccounted for and that they were probably dead on the field of battle. They had no problem in escaping the Mexican Cavalry and successfully reached Juh's stronghold. There they had teamed up with the warriors under Juh, consisting of several Netdahes, two Navajos, three Mexican renegades, a dozen Chiracahuas, and about twenty-five Chihenne and Bedonkohe Apaches under Geronimo.

Apache Tears

CHAPTER FIVE

Pack Train Captured

Lozen rested a week after reaching the Netdahe stronghold. And then just as she was becoming weary of doing nothing, she was called to confer with Juh and Geronimo. They were concerned that there were Warm Springs and other Apaches scattered throughout the Black Range that hadn't received the message to retreat to the stronghold in Mexico.

They asked Lozen and two warriors to make a trip to the Black Range in order to locate any stragglers and let them know where the main band had gone. Two more warriors were to initially accompany them and then split to the east to reconnoiter the situation at San Carlos and Camp Apache where they were to deliver the message that, soon, they would be called upon to leave the reservation and join their independent brethren.

Lozen was happy with the assignment. She had had all of the camp life she wanted. She longed to be in the field fighting for the Apache's cause. The warriors with her were the finest in the band and shared Lozen's eagerness to again be on an important mission. The group of five left the mountaintop and descended down the zigzag trail heading east crossing the valleys and ridges until they were southwest of Janos. They were afraid Mexican cavalry would be posted along the more direct trails from the stronghold to the U.S. border.

They reached a point on a ridge overlooking the canyon where they had been besieged. There, they camped for the night. Lozen advised against lighting any fires in such an open location and then admitted to her comrades that she had a premonition that they were in danger, and that they should be doubly alert during the night. While the warriors respected Lozen's powers, they placed no credence in the foreboding she felt as they were on the high ground and had seen nothing to cause them any alarm.

Ten minutes later one of the warriors exclaimed, "Look to the plain! There is a camp fire, and there, another."

Before long there were twelve fires burning in the dusk of evening, which signified a large group of people, possibly a military expedition. Lozen and her companions slept fitfully throughout the night, anxious for the sunrise so they could see who was camped below them.

The dawn finally came and, in the light, the Apaches could see that it was indeed a military expedition of about two hundred men who appeared to be dressed in regular Mexican cavalry uniforms and a group of fifteen irregulars who, after camp was broken, were observed escorting the baggage train.

The cavalry unit headed north and Lozen told her companions, "They are headed on the trail that intercepts our usual passageway to the Blue Mountains."

All agreed that was indeed their goal, and when they saw that the pack train was heading directly up the draw, they realized that it was being sent on a more direct route to meet with the cavalry later on.

Lozen saw a golden opportunity and turned to her companions exclaiming, "I think we should ambush such a juicy gift, maybe they are the ones," she said in jest, "that gave us so much grief at this very place."

Again everyone agreed and immediately they descended to the canyon with two of the warriors on the lower eastern end, two on the higher western end, with Lozen in the middle. They were on the south side of the canyon which had the lower bank. This would pin the Mexicans inside if the trap worked.

During one of Lozen's reunions with her kinsman, Geronimo was so happy to see her that the presented her with an almost new, latest model, Winchester repeating carbine. It was a gun that Geronimo had taken in a recent raid and it was the envy of every Apache in the camp. With this and a buckskin pouch of two hundred bullets, Lozen was ready for a good fight.

With the Mexicans just a hundred yards away, the Apaches could hear the bell of the lead mule clanging and the banter of the soldiers as they rode along with the pack train. Quickly, they came into view. Lozen's heart commenced to pound. There, leading the train, was the very Mexican who had tried to rape her.

As the rest of the riders hove into view, she quickly identified other men who had raped her niece and the other woman. The emotional impact of seeing these hated men within rifle range would have enraged many to the point of being less effective, but not Lozen. As her anger welled within her, her nerves calmed even more. She clamped her teeth tight, permitting a vicious smile to appear on her face as she relished the penance she was about to exact.

Lozen's plan was that the two warriors on the west end would open fire as soon as the riders had cleared their position. This would spur everyone up the canyon directly into the fire of the others. Lozen had speculated that they would have no recourse but to charge into the direct fire of the Apaches as the embankment on the other side was too high for horses to jump.

Just then, two sharp cracks of rifle fire opened the battle and two Mexicans immediately fell from their saddles. The others did exactly as Lozen had predicted and headed up the canyon at a full gallop. They were immediately in Lozen's sights. With three quick shots, three more Mexicans were on the ground. They came into the range of the two warriors on the west who opened with a devastating fire, leaving only four of the twelve pack guards alive. Those instantly wheeled towards the lower bank hoping to escape the deadly cross fire. Two of them came directly at Lozen. She leveled her carbine at the horsemen rapidly approaching her and squeezed a shot off just before she recognized the bestial face of her tormentor in her sights. Her bullet split his skull wide open. She quickly levered another shell in the chamber and killed his companion. Two others passed above Lozen and successfully escaped into the chaparral.

As Lozen lowered her carbine and looked at the bodies sprawled some thirty feet in front of her, she heard a victory cry to her left and knew that the ambush had been a success. Only two of the Mexicans had survived. The pack train had scattered up the canyon. The Apaches spent thirty minutes securing the animals and then quickly stripped the dead men of their weapons and started back trailing to the west. They were worried that perhaps the main column had been close enough to hear the sound of their firing. When they reached the ridge in back of them, they could look out and see a great deal of the Chihuahuan Plains. The main group was not in view. The Apaches agreed that they were probably safe for the time being.

The group excitedly recounted the battle with each other and was amazed when, one by one, they all said that they had heard not one single shot fired by the Mexican guards. The victors were too anxious to clear out to determine what the pack train included but it had to be military supplies and it was essential that they get them back to Geronimo and Juh.

Lozen took it upon herself to change the plan of their mission.

She told her comrades, "It is best that you go back. All four of you will be needed to control this many animals and you may very well be trailed by the main force of the Mexicans. I will carry on the mission to the Black Range and, when it is finished, I will visit our brethren on the reservation as I will be less of a suspect to the white-eyes than any of you."

Lozen had not been placed in formal charge of the group as the leaders did not want to offend the Apache tradition of male dominance. They had individually asked each of the warriors to listen carefully to the advice of Lozen who all knew was a possessor of great powers. When Lozen set out her plan, all agreed, delighted to be headed back to the stronghold with such a valuable treasure. They immediately left along the route they had come while Lozen struck off alone to the north towards the Black Range.

Apache Tears

CHAPTER SIX

Snakebite

When Lozen parted with her companions, she headed north along the ridgeline which formed the header from which the ambush canyon descended. After ten miles of quick travel, she was at a point where the ridge began to slope to the north and there she could see to the northwest the cloud of dust being raised by the main Mexican force. They were still traveling northwest so obviously they had not been made aware of the fate of their supplies.

Confident that there were no other troops in the vicinity, Lozen quickened her pace and for the next ten hours alternated between walking at a fast gait or resorting to the Apache trot. Lozen could easily, in twenty-four hours, outdistance a horse at this pace and the soles of her moccasins would wear out before she would.

She made good time, reaching the U.S. border to the south of Stein's Pass. However, in order to avoid any military contingent that might be stationed there, she decided to bypass it to the east. In order to do so, she had to cross a rocky canyon. Half way up the far side, she reached with her left hand over a rock jutting out from a ledge.

As she started to climb upward, she thought of the possibility of a rattler being concealed in the rocks but put the thought out of her mind, focusing all her concentration on the difficult physical task of climbing. Her lapse of concern cost her dearly as she felt the searing pain of a rattler's fangs tearing into her left forearm. It was a big Timber Rattler that had struck the muscle of her arm.

Lozen reached over with her right hand, grabbed the snake in back of its jaws and, tearing it loose, threw it back over her head into the canyon below. She lifted herself up onto the ledge where the snake had been lodged and began sucking on the wound. As she did this, she used her right hand to apply pressure above the injury. She knew from the lore of the old ones that the more venom you could remove immediately, the better chance you had for survival. She also knew that in spite of this immediate application of first aid, she was in for a rough time and possibly faced death.

She recalled the old Apache adage, *Be fast before the snake strikes, and then be slow.*

Apache tradition told all of the young people that the worst thing to do after a snakebite was to run or walk, that you should be still and avoid all exertion. Lozen continued to suck on the wound as she settled herself on the ledge for a long wait.

By nightfall, the wound began to swell ominously: First the forearm, and then the upper arm, and then the shoulder. The skin of her forehead was beginning to feel tight and from her dry mouth, she knew she was running a high fever. Tied by a thong to her waistband was a deer's bladder full of water. She used this sparingly, knowing that she might be on the ledge for several days while the poison attacked her body. Shortly after dusk, she lost consciousness and slept without wakening throughout the night. It was almost noon the next day before she regained consciousness and saw that her left arm had continued to swell. The puncture wounds themselves were now festering and she knew she must keep the wounds clean to avoid further infection.

There was a small Agave plant growing from a fissure on the ledge where she was perched. She was able to move her tortured body over to it and cut off one of the thick stubby leaves. This she split with her knife and used, along with some dry grass, as a compress on the punctures. In the meantime, to conserve her water supply, she placed pebbles in her mouth, rolling them around and sucking on them as she drifted in and out of merciful sleep. She had done everything she could do. The rest was in the hands of Ussen who would take her now if that were his will.

With no misgiving or remorse, satisfied that she had always been true to the Apache code and honored her people, she drifted into a deep sleep, not to awaken for two days. When she did, she realized she had shifted during her sleep to the very edge of the ledge and would have fallen over had she moved another inch.

After apprising herself of where she was, she realized that she was sweating profusely. She looked at her arm and could see that the swelling had gone down some. The site of the punctures, however, was a different story. They were more inflamed than before with the flesh putrefying around the bite. She knew that this now was her greatest problem and that the venom was probably losing its strength. She also knew what had to be done and immediately started a fire with some grass and big thorn cactus growing out of crevices on the ledge.

When the fire was burning bright, she fixed her eyes on the dancing flames and asked for Ussen's intervention. She held her knife in the hot blaze, turning it until the tip was cherry red. She quickly excised the rotten flesh on her forearm, cutting into the good flesh throughout the area of the infection. She repeatedly put her knife back in the fire, knowing that the red-hot heat would keep the blood from flowing too freely. Even though she was cauterizing the capillaries and vessels, there was still profuse bleeding and when she was finished she cut another Agave leaf and used it as a poultice. Continuing to sweat heavily, Lozen changed the poultice every half-hour and by noon of the fourth day, she began to believe that she might indeed survive her ordeal.

That night, as she slept fitfully, her whole life passed in review. The happy days as a child, competing with her brother and her friends in the athletic games that all Apaches enjoyed, sitting around the campfire, listening to the stories of the elders about Apache bravery and honor, and enjoying the beautiful countryside from which Ussen gave them the tools of life. How wonderful it had all been. Then the terrible invasion of the white-eyes, their mistreatment of the Indians, their greed in wanting the Indian's lands, and their lies and false-promises. She had fully agreed with the decision of the Chiefs to stand up and fight back, but she was wondering, *Where will it all end.*

Her brother, Victorio, the greatest of all Apache Chiefs had fallen to the Mexicans at Tres Castillos. Mangas Colorado had been tricked and brutally murdered. Cochise had been abused by a young Army lieutenant from West Point who had killed Apaches under a false truce. Juh, Geronimo, and Nana were the only leaders left who were fighting the white-eyes. There were some fine warriors still in the field, but they were outnumbered a thousand to one. They would make great Chiefs some day if they could but survive. Sadly, she now realized that was an impossibility. But what choice was there? To go live at the San Carlos Reservation in the dung pile of the Calvary - that was worse than eternal hell. No, she thought, *It is better to defend the altar fire of Apache faith and die an Indian, an Apache, a true believer in the ways of Ussen.*

It seemed to Lozen that it was only yesterday that this horrible ordeal had begun with the escape across the Mal Pais. As she drifted to sleep, her thoughts returned to the aftermath of the Warm Springs rejection of the San Carlos Reservation.

CHAPTER SEVEN

Across the Mal Pais

Two years after the Warm Springs had been forcibly removed to San Carlos, a few families slipped off the reservation and reoccupied their old haunts at Ojos Caliente. When the army took no action against them, more and more of the Warm Springs were encouraged to leave the dreaded San Carlos country and return to their homeland. Victorio, Geronimo, and Nana were among these. By Victorio's side was his sister, Lozen.

There was great fear that the cavalry would someday fall upon the refugees and attack them. Victorio had instructed everyone to keep a supply of food and a blanket on hand at all times and to be prepared to scatter. Assignments had been made to families and individuals as to where they would go if attacked and how they would rendezvous after the danger had passed. The main purpose of the plan was to give the women and children a chance to reach the security of the Sacramento Mountains and their cousins, the Mescaleros.

Victorio placed Lozen in charge of this phase of the retreat. Plans were made with the various women to bring the children with them to a series of rendezvous points before reaching the Rio Grande.

Twice San Carlos Apache scouts visited the encampment with warnings that the patience of the whites was wearing thin and that if they did not return immediately, their camp would be attacked and there would be no survivors. A month after the last warning the threat was carried out. Just before dawn, three troops of cavalry fell on the Ojos Caliente encampment. Two families were camped at the site of the old fort and the soldiers mistakenly believed from the various campfires they maintained that this was the main body. In fact it was a ruse, a diversionary tactic frequently employed by the Apaches to disguise the camp's real location.

At the first sounds of shots and cries of alarm, Lozen gathered three orphan children who were staying in her wickiup and started towards the box of the Canada Alamosa. The jumble of jagged rocks below the water line would make it difficult for the cavalry to follow. Soon the narrow confines of the box were crowded with Indian women and children making their way downstream.

A group of warriors had camped a quarter of a mile away from the main encampment and maintained a rigid rule of no fires. At the first sound of battle, they grouped and fell upon the rear of the cavalry as the dawn was breaking. The cavalry had annihilated the families who had set up the false camp and quickly turned to meet this threat from their rear. While they outnumbered the Warm Springs three to one they were slowly forced back by the ferocity of the Indian charge. As daylight quickened, the soldiers with their better weapons were able to gain the advantage and Victorio signaled a retreat. As the warriors fell back, they did so in small groups, scattering in every direction.

The cavalry broke into smaller units and futilely tried to follow the Indians as they drifted into the rocks and brush that covered the hills around Ojos Caliente. The warriors had abandoned their mounts and were scrambling on foot over the rough mountainside. The cavalry tried to follow on their horses but soon found that there was no way for them to keep up the pace in such difficult terrain. One by one they abandoned their mounts and continued to press after the Apaches on foot only to find their elusive quarry could travel at twice their speed. As the two groups toiled up the hillsides, the Apaches rallied and began setting ambushes for groups of two and three soldiers foolish enough to press forward, not realizing that the Apaches were on their home ground.

Lieutenant Tramine, in charge of the three troops, had the bugler sound recall when he saw that what had started out to be a victory was quickly becoming a major defeat. The soldiers responded with both speed and appreciation. They had had their fill of fighting the Apaches even though they badly outnumbered them.

Groups of women and children traveled through the box and then scattered to various sanctuaries where they took refuge until the next night when, in independent groups, they resumed their journey. Some went down the ridges that rose precipitously on each side of the Canada Alamosa while others headed more to the north and others to the south down the Cuchillo Negro draw.

Lozen, with her great physical strength, had pressed rapidly forward, locating groups at various rendezvous points and urging them to continue their flight. Some of the children had failed to heed the warnings of the elders and had left camp without water, food, or blankets. Lozen told them where goods and supplies were cached in secret caves, just for such emergencies. She also managed to raid several small farmsteads in the Cuchillo Negro valley. Even though these people had been friendly to the Indians, there was no course open but to steal food and clothing in such an emergency.

After doing as much as she could to be sure that everyone was on their way, she went back to a cave halfway up the left side of the Canada Alamosa where she had left her three young charges. She had been gone for over twenty-four hours. Fearful that she would frighten the children, she called softly from the ledge below the cave, "It is I, Lozen. Do not be alarmed."

A tiny voice replied, "We are not afraid, Lozen. Come quickly."

Lozen entered the cave and gave the children strips of jerky meat that she had taken from clotheslines. She cut the meat into small squares so that the children could manage it and gave them each a drink of water. They had all left the camp with dried corn and venison prepared as pemmican and each had brought a blanket.

The next day at nightfall, Lozen gathered her group and quickly made for the Rio Grande. They traveled hard all through the night with Lozen alternately carrying the three small children. Lozen stopped when they reached the valley floor and, secreting the children in a clump of Mesquite, quickly located four other groups who were waiting for her in sanctuaries. With this large group she pressed southward, stopping at the mouth of a large side canyon where she located two more groups. They now numbered some forty women and children and two old men. Lozen exhorted them all to press forward and not one voice was raised in pain or protest as they struggled through the night, gashing their legs on Lechuguilla cactus and falling on rock and tearing their clothing in a headlong race to reach the river and avoid the cavalry troops that they knew would be scouring the whole country in search of the apostates.

When they reached the traditional river crossing, Lozen was relieved to find both Nana and Victorio already there, hidden in a dense grove of cottonwood. They had gathered another twenty women and children. As they prepared to cross the river, Tis-ta-dae came riding in with a group of five warriors and another fifteen refugees and a remuda of 20 head. There were five women and a dozen children not accounted for.

Victorio said a prayer to Ussen and gave the order to placate the river and cross at once. Everyone, including the children, who had any turquoise on them promptly cast it into the river and all could see the flash of blue along the line of Apaches as they waited to brave the current.

Lozen had a large mule that had been given to her by Tis-ta-dae and, with two of her charges aboard, was the first to plunge into the water and quickly reach the other bank. Soon all of the women and children were safely across and waving at the men on the opposite shore before heading for the San Andreas range. A few of the women stayed behind with the men to help them in their campaign against the whites by keeping camp, tending the horses, and, if need be, fighting by their sides.

Lozen, with her charges, including a few elderly, double mounted and in some cases, four children on an animal, pushed towards Salinas Peak, the sacred mountain, and the trail that led between the Mal Pais and the gypsum white sands. They traveled all night crossing the San Andreas and at dawn camped huddled in the Mal Pais for cover. They could see faint clouds of dust to the south of them as cavalry units were crossing the Organ Pass heading west to reinforce the troops which had been bested by the Apaches at the battle of Ojos Caliente.

When nightfall came, Lozen gathered all of the refugees about her and told them, "We now are going to go through the most dangerous part of our mission. I know you want to stay on the horses but we are going to turn them loose now because the cavalry will find us for sure if we remain mounted. We must cross the Mal Pais at night and your moccasins will be torn to shreds. Your feet will be raw and bleeding but we must press on."

Lozen paused and then continued, "We cannot stay on the trail, because I fear there are cavalry units everywhere and they will seek out the usual trails. If they do, we could blunder directly into them so we are going to travel through the Mal Pais and try to skirt them by morning."

No one complained even though they all knew the tortures their bodies were going to go through in order to avoid the cavalry units.

As the night progressed, moccasins were torn to shreds and those without replacements proceeded on raw and bloody feet. Lozen found a girl of twelve sitting by the side of the trail, unable to move on and looking to her feet, saw that she had serious wounds. Lozen took off her tunic and, tearing it in two, wrapped it about the girl's feet and tied two strips of buckskin thong to hold the make shift footgear in place.

She urged the girl, "Stand up now. You must go on. You can do it."

The girl, with tears in her eyes, nodded her head yes and limped forward, following the others passing by. Lozen went up and down the line, even though her own moccasins were in tatters, telling the women to use their tunics and whatever they could to wrap around the feet of the children so they could continue.

The emergency repairs did the job and by morning they were through the volcanic formation and were resting. They camped at the edge of the lava beds in deep grottos where they were protected and screened so they could nurse their injured limbs. Everyone pooled their food and shared equally in the meager rations that were left. Lozen asked the two old men who were with them, "Can you take charge and keep everyone quiet and hidden until I can reconnoiter and see what is the best approach to the Sacramentos?" The old men nodded their assent.

Lozen left the makeshift camp and sped like an antelope down a low draw, crouching so as not to be seen. She was quickly out on the desert floor where she rapidly worked her way along dry streambeds and arroyos until she, at last, reached Dog Canyon. She was delighted to find that there were no troops camped there and she quickly scouted a mile or so up the canyon then returned to her charges. She had covered some forty miles on foot without moccasins in rough country and yet, when she returned to the women and children, she was ready at once to start out on the trip to Dog Canyon.

Half way out onto the desert floor, Lozen, in the lead, suddenly froze and dropped to the ground. Everyone followed suit. Lozen had a premonition of danger. She softly told the women immediately behind her to pass the word to remain still and hidden while she scouted ahead. She had gone scarcely a quarter of a mile when she heard the sound of horses. She froze beside a large rock as a troop of cavalry, Pueblo Scouts leading them, passed between her and her charges. She was terrified when she saw that there were Indians with them and that they were frequently stopping and bending to the ground to look for signs.

They only stopped occasionally and by good luck missed all signs of Lozen's passage both then and earlier. The cavalry was headed on an angle from the direction Lozen had struck and passed within a hundred feet of the huddled refugees. The soldiers were obviously moving north to cut off any retreat of Apaches from the Black Range. Later, Lozen speculated to one of the older man, "Surely they did not know about the trail around the sacred mountain or that's where they would have gone."

Lozen was wrong. They did know about that trail and another troop of cavalry was, at that very moment, passing along it over the San Andreas Range heading west with Pueblo scouts excitedly following the path of the animals that Lozen had abandoned when they started out on foot through the Mal Pais.

When the animals were turned loose, Lozen had told everyone to hit them with sticks and throw rocks at them to get them moving up the trail, hoping that this would convince anyone who came along that Apaches were ahead of them moving westward. The ruse worked perfectly otherwise the cavalry troop that was chasing the unmounted animals would have picked up the trail of the refugees had they not been decoyed. When the soldier's had passed, Lozen hurried her charges along, knowing that there might well be other troops moving during the night to establish blockades and prevent the Apaches' escape.

It took the entire night for Lozen to lead her bedraggled group across the desert floor to the mouth of Dog Canyon. Here she took them up a side canyon and pointed out a cave which they could reach by handholds. The cavalry had never found this hiding place which had been used by Indians who lived in the area long before the Apaches. Lozen asked the two old men to take charge of the group while she went for emergency food. There was ample water from a cool spring in the bottom of the small canyon and Lozen told the refugees, "No more than one person at a time should go down to the spring to provide water for the rest. If soldiers appear, you will have to surrender to avoid disclosing the hiding place of the others."

Lozen and two young women who had just recently passed through their ceremonies of maidenhood hurried up the floor of Dog Canyon and by noon were in the pine forests. Lozen had not slept for two days and realized that her strength was beginning to leave her. The girls were cousins of Lozen. One was named Fawn

Skin and the other Gentle Moon. Lozen guided them to a promontory where there was good visibility of the full length of Dog Canyon below and gave them instructions on searching for help from the Mescalero.

She sent Fawn Skin to the north towards Sierra Blanca while Gentle Moon was sent due east to look in the canyons for rancherias of Mescalero.

Gentle Moon returned before the sun was down with a group of six Mescalero hunters and a deer they had killed. Lozen had piled some rocks pointing in the direction of Dog Canyon. The rocks were used as a sign to Fawn Skin that the group had returned down the canyon and that they were to follow.

The Mescalero men pushed ahead and overtook Lozen who explained where the group was hidden. The men, traveling by moonlight, reached the refugees before midnight. It was well past the middle of the night when Lozen and Gentle Moon finally came in and another two hours before Fawn Skin appeared with three women she had found gathering pinons. They had two baskets of the pine fruit with them.

There was great happiness as everyone ate their fill but Lozen warned that they would hide out for the day and continue the next night despite the horrible condition of the feet of the children and adults. The Mescaleros who befriended them had a few extra pairs of moccasins with them and they shared their clothing to make emergency footgear. As the sun went down that afternoon, the band made its way up Dog Canyon and then deep into the Sacramentos to the security of a rancheria located on a sparkling stream. It had been a miraculous journey through the heart of army patrols through some of the most rugged country that existed anywhere. Arms and legs were gashed and bleeding and the soles of many feet were red pulp but there were no fatalities. Everyone had made it safely.

The Mescaleros spread the word throughout the Sacramentos that a large group of Warm Springs women and children had taken refuge with them and two warriors were dispatched to find Victorio and let him know that Lozen had gotten through.

CHAPTER EIGHT

Children Rescued

On the fifth day after the snakebite, Lozen began to concentrate on the present. The swelling was greatly diminished, and Lozen could move her arm easily. The poultices were having their effect and the drainage had been reduced to only an ooze. A scab was beginning to form where the flesh had been cut away.

Lozen finished the last of her canteen water and munched on some dried venison and corn, making plans to start the next day toward the Black Range. When the dawn broke on the sixth day, Lozen was ready to continue on and, with no difficulty, completed her climb out of the canyon to the top of the canyon wall.

She moved straight north, taking advantage of every defile and clump of rocks so as not to be easily seen by anyone on the lookout from the heights above. By dark she was north of the El Paso-California road and moving across the desert towards the Burro Mountains. She traveled rapidly and by midnight was well into the Burros where she camped in a clump of Yucca.

She had gone without food for a day but had replenished her canteen at a spring on the southern slopes of the Burro Mountains.

She was up at dawn and gathered half a dozen green tunas, the fruit of the flat-bladed Nopal cactus. Although it was green, it gave nourishment, and permitted her to go on. As she did, she kept her sling, made of leather thongs and used for hunting small game, ever ready, not daring to risk a shot, as she was nearing the mining area now thickly populated with whites.

Her opportunity came when a small Cottontail jumped up at her feet and scurried ahead. With two sweeps of her sling, she let a rock fly, hitting the rabbit in the back of the head, killing it instantly. She found herself a small cave in the side of a canyon wall and risked building a fire in order to eat her first real meal in eight days. She laid the rabbit on the burning embers once the fire had died out and sprinkled it generously with salt she had in another pouch. The meat turned black, but when the crust was peeled away, the flesh was juicy and tender. She devoured the rabbit and lay back in her shelter to rest for an hour.

Refreshed and restored, Lozen moved on quickly, passing the Silver City to Mogollon road. Here she moved due north into the Mogollons and struck the west fork of the Gila River. She went down the west fork and then up the east fork, branching off to Diamond Creek where she headed toward its headwaters in the Black Range.

For the next two weeks, Lozen methodically visited each rendezvous point which she had been directed to reconnoiter, and was able to locate thirty Apaches who were hiding and not aware of where the band had gone. Most of them were women and children, happy to learn there were still Chihenne Apaches alive.

Lozen instructed them on their route and sent them on their way to the Blue Mountain stronghold in the heart of the Sierra Madre. As soon as Lozen bid farewell to this group, she struck to the north and during the night, passed through Ojos Caliente with heavy heart. It was here that both she and Victorio had been born.

For the next week she searched through the San Mateos range finding no Apaches until she reached the final sanctuary. As she neared this last hiding point, she could smell smoke and knew that someone was there. She also had a strong premonition of danger but sensed that she herself was not the person in peril. She took every precaution as she approached the cave about fifteen feet above the canyon bottom. Using a series of hand and foot holes, she reached the clearing in front of the cave. Once there, she saw the reason for her premonition. A pack of five grey Lobo wolves were lying below in the canyon. Four of them were asleep and the fifth was gazing balefully at the ledge of the cliff where a small fire was burning.

Lozen could make out the figures of children huddled against the side of the cave protected by a pile of rocks about them. There was one adult with the children. She was an old woman who could not be of much help if the wolves attacked. The wolves, however, were in no hurry. They knew their quarry was weakening without food or water. But they also knew from prior experience that men were very ingenious and could throw rocks and fight like hell when cornered. They were content to wait their prey out and enjoy their feast without incurring any wounds themselves.

The guard wolf either scented Lozen or had a power of his own as he suddenly turned his head and stared directly at her, emitting a guttural growl of warning. The pack immediately were on their feet and all faced towards Lozen. She knew that if she hesitated for a second they would rip her apart and so, without hesitation, she charged, yelling like an army of Apaches with her knife poised high in her right hand.

Lozen's act of courage paid big dividends as each wolf scattered away on his own, running as if it were the one for whom Lozen intended the blade. Lozen quickly was inside the cave accepting the welcome of her Apache brethren. When the wolves began to reappear one at a time, Lozen stood on the ledge and, using her sling, began to deal them misery. A rock from Lozen's sling, hurtling along could cause a big headache. Three of the wolves, being hit on the skull, promptly abandoned their meal plans. As they left the scene, their companions joined them and all were soon out of sight, thinking to hunt easier prey than this amazing human possessing such accuracy.

The old woman with the children told Lozen that they had been on their own for at least two weeks, that the parents of the children had gone to steal food from the farms of the white-eyes in the Rio Grande Valley. They had never returned and all feared that they were dead.

Lozen warned them, "We must leave here immediately. If your parents come back, they will know we have gone. I will leave a marker for them."

She arranged pebbles in a row pointing south towards Mexico with the smaller pebbles indicating the direction of travel. She had to goad her frightened charges on the trail back towards Ojos Caliente.

Lozen had been using her sling to kill rabbits and provide her little group with food when she decided to take a chance on the use of her rifle. She killed a mature ten-point buck. She cooked the meat the same way she cooked rabbit, leaving the skin on and putting the carcass on a bed of coals. It was the first food other than pemmican the children and old lady had had for several days. Everyone gorged on the rare meal and went to sleep that night feeling better about themselves and life than they had for a long time.

After two days travel they reached Ojos Caliente which Lozen skirted cautiously to the north and west, remembering the old adage that "when water is here, danger is near."

She gathered her charges and explained, "We are going to head towards the land of the Bedonkohe on the headwaters of the Gila. I know there are no Indians left in the Black Range, but perhaps on the Gila tributaries we may find someone who can help us reach the stronghold in Mexico."

They climbed due west, crossing the continental divide, then traveled along a ridge that gradually descended into the Gila Basin. Here they passed through an open mountain glade near the headwaters of the east fork of the Gila. They continued east, skirting the northern edges of Black Mountain and then dropped to the south down a deep escarpment into a place called "The Meadows." The Meadows, on the middle fork, was a favorite summer camp of the

Bedonkohe Apache band.

There was no sign of recent Indian activity in this area. Lozen moved up the Middle Fork with her little group, hoping to find signs of occupation. They traveled to the headwaters and then up Willow Creek without finding any trace of Apache presence. As they passed under the brow of Loco Mountain, Lozen paused and told her charges that they were at the summer camp where both Geronimo and Juh had been born.

By the time the little band had topped out at Nickel Creek Divide, Lozen was sure that there were no Apaches left in the Gila or the Mogollons. She also speculated that it would be a difficult task, without assistance, to shepherd a group to Mexico so debilitated both by youth and old age, as were her charges. She realized, *The only sensible thing I can do is take them to the reservation at San Carlos. They will only be a burden at the Netdahe stronghold.*

She announced her decision with great regret. The youngsters all wanted to go to Mexico on the belief that their mothers and fathers might be there.

Lozen counseled them, "No, my children. They would not go there voluntarily and leave you behind. But if they have been captured, they may be at San Carlos and that's where we're going."

Half a day above the juncture of Canyon Creek on the Middle Fork, Lozen led her little party into a beautiful meadow where a trail came down from the escarpment to the North. This was a favorite summer spot of the Bedonkohe band. The canyon was secluded here and offered good protection from the weather. Anyone coming at them from above would make a real racket, dislodging the rocks as they came down the steep trail. Lozen decided that they would spend two days here to let her charges rest before they resumed their journey.

Lozen was busy using her sling on the local rabbits and even managed to catch three half-grown turkey poults. As a result, they ate sumptuously. Lozen dried the meat that was left over for their journey to Arizona.

They resumed their journey early in the morning. When

negotiating a steep bank around a beaver dam, Lozen fell behind to help the old lady who was having trouble struggling up the bank. Lozen heard a terrified scream and turned to see what was the matter. Since the children were out of view, Lozen bounded up the bank drawing her knife.

Thirty feet away was a large mountain lion mauling the oldest child. Lozen rushed forward and pounced on the lion's back, plunging her knife repeatedly into its chest. The lion let the child go, twisting violently trying to free itself from this unexpected attack. When it attempted to turn and confront Lozen, she plunged her knife deep into its throat slitting the jugular. The lion struggled feverishly for a moment in a death throe and then went limp.

Lozen looked for the wounded child who had joined the others back on the trail. Lozen checked the girl over, as well as herself, and found that while they had some wounds, none were serious. They spent two hours at the site treating the cuts and recovering their composure.

When all was more or less back to normal, Lozen examined the lion. It was a huge male whose coat was splotched and frayed. It was covered with the scars of many battles and conquests but was ill equipped to fend for itself in the wild. Its incisor teeth were broken off. It only had two claws left on one front pad and none on the other.

While a formidable opponent for a person, this lion was obviously not able to stalk and kill its normal prey of Mule Deer and Elk. It had been reduced to scavenging the carrion of others and picking up an occasional easy mark like a porcupine or, in this case, a young girl. Where the lion had attacked the girl, there was a large boulder just two feet from the trail, which lay between the boulder and the bank of the stream. It was an easy ambush and, no doubt, had been the scene of many successful kills.

After this scare, the group stayed tightly together, close to Lozen, as they made their way westward towards Arizona and the San Carlos Reservation. After the incident with the lion, every night when they camped, before they went to sleep, Lozen taught the children about the tricks of surviving in the wilderness. She chided the twelve-year-old girl who had almost been killed and told her to always walk in the wild with the eye of the predator and to constantly be thinking of where you would be and what you would do if you were trying to make a meal of a young Apache girl coming down the trail.

She also explained the healing properties of the Nopal cactus leaf and how to use it as a compress and told them how to treat the bite of a snake and, most importantly, the art of setting bones and the use of splints. She also gave some helpful hints on navigation and pointed out the fixed star that did not move and told them that Ussen had placed it in the sky to serve as a beacon for a young Apache girl who was lost in the forest. A child who had wandered away from her parents while hunting pinons was hopelessly confused and couldn't find her way back to their camp and she fell asleep from exhaustion. Then Ussen, in her dreams, told her to look to the star and follow it to safety. The girl followed Ussen's directions and was saved and Ussen left the star there as an aid to all other Apaches who might be lost.

After a good night's sleep, the band struck out for the lower reaches of the Gila River and the Indian reservation where the Southern Apache bands were being forced to congregate. It took four days to drop down from the high mountains of the Mogollons to the low deserts of San Carlos but her little band made it without event. Lozen hid in some rocks a mile from the agency office while she watched her charges march across the desert floor and report to the Indian Agent that they wished his protection.

After seeing that the charges were safely inside the agency office, Lozen hid out for the rest of the day, then spent her evenings for the next week visiting as many of the Apache family groups as she could, eventually reaching Camp Apache. Each family that Lozen visited told her the same thing. The conditions were terrible and rumors were everywhere that they were going to be put on trial by the Arizona authorities or shipped to prison in the East. They told a tale of brutal treatment by the Indian scouts themselves who lorded over them and had become stooges for the white-eyes. They also warned Lozen that there were spies in every camp and to be careful because the scouts would shoot her on sight if they saw her.

Every Apache with whom Lozen talked told her of an Apache messiah Noch-ay-del-Kline, who was called the "Dreamer." The "Dreamer" claimed that he had the power to summon the dead. Lozen's informants told her that the dead Chiefs were speaking through the "Dreamer", urging the Apaches to rise up and force the invaders from their lands.

Anxious to carry news of the new messiah, Lozen started back to the stronghold in the Blue Mountains. When she left the San Carlos Reservation, four young Apache men - two Warm Springs and two Chiricahua - accompanied her. At fifteen years of age, they had all just recently gone through their inductions into manhood and were anxious to begin training as warriors. Their families had consented with great misgivings to them leaving but they had great confidence in Lozen.

Lozen decided that, unhindered by women and children, they would take the direct route back and she struck across the desert for the stronghold, traveling at night. Within three days they were in the foothills of the Sierra Madre. In another day they were across the Bavispe River and beginning the ascent of the zigzag trail to the mountaintop.

Some Apaches who were ensconced above them since they entered the bottom of the canyon kept a careful watch over Lozen and her little band. They became a welcoming committee waiting for them.

One of the warriors Lozen particularly felt close to was Tis-ta-dae who had been fighting beside Nana since the initial outbreak. He called down to Lozen as she neared the top of the trail and asked her to identify herself. Lozen stopped and was puzzled for a minute and then realized it was her comrade who was challenging her in jest.

She called back, "Beware, I am a soldier of the white-eyes and I have come to catch you Apaches and teach you a lesson."

Tis-ta-dae stood up on the rock on which he was perched and

shouted down to Lozen, "Come and catch me then white-eyes, I'll show you how easy it is to find an Apache."

With that taunt, he sped towards the main camp with Lozen in hot pursuit. As he raced into the main camp, Tis-ta-dae saw Nana sitting on a log shaping some fire sticks.

He ran over to his mentor and sat beside him imploring, "Nantan Nana, protect me. There is a white-eyes out to capture all Apaches."

Just then Lozen raced into view, coming to a halt in front of the taciturn Chief who looked up wryly and said, "You are the strangest looking white-eyes I have ever seen. Where have you been my daughter? We have worried about you for two months now!"

Lozen sat down on the log on the other side of Nana and began to tell all she had seen and done. As she spoke an audience gathered around her. She told of her part in the capture of the pack train; the ordeal with the snakebite; and the encounter with the wolves. She then told her audience what the situation was in San Carlos. In the middle of her report on San Carlos, Geronimo joined the crowd sitting on the log beside Lozen. He listened intently and asked her many questions about how many soldiers she had seen and if the Indians at San Carlos were in condition to travel great distances and fight. She told him, "No, they are not. They are poorly fed. They are ill-equipped and at a low ebb of spirit."

Geronimo shook his head sadly back and forth and then brightened and thanked Lozen for so faithfully discharging her mission. She asked where Juh was and was told he had gone into Janos in spite of the warnings of everyone. He enjoyed special status with the people at Janos and, every once in a while, would go there to replenish his supply of mescal. Nana was especially displeased at Juh's visit to the Mexican city. Geronimo only regretted that his friends had talked him out of accompanying Juh in his quest for the Mexican poison.

When Geronimo learned that Lozen had brought four young warriors back with her, he asked that they be brought forward so that he could inspect them. He was very pleased that Lozen had brought additions, albeit young ones, to his fighting forces and quickly assigned the boys to older Indians for their training lessons.

Lozen had saved for the end her startling news about the visions of Noch-ay-del-Kline and she stunned all with her information, "There is a man of great powers talking to the dead chiefs and enlisting their aid in restoring the Apaches to our homeland." She detailed all she had heard about the "Dreamer" and his power to summon the dead. Everyone was fascinated by this unusual news which could affect Apache destiny in a positive way.

That night as Lozen drifted to sleep she recalled the joy of her return to the stronghold and in particular the comic welcome of Tis-ta-dae.

She thought, *if I were just now fifteen years old, that is the man I think I could accept. He is strong and daring, but respectful to everyone. He believes in the Apache ways. He is just what Victorio would have selected for me. But he is too young and it is too late, and I have no choice now but to go on and work Ussen's will.*

As she fell asleep she fantasized that the impediments did not exist and that she and Tis-ta-dae were man and wife. Unknown to Lozen, not fifty feet away in a wickiup shared with Nana, Tis-ta-dae was dreaming quietly, wondering what he would do if Lozen would show any interest in him. He thought, *she is much older but that is no impediment. I don't feel the passion of love but I have a strong bond towards this Apache woman warrior who is the equal of any man in the Apache cause. Well, it doesn't matter. I have a job to do and it doesn't include marriage or a family. Not until our lands have been returned and once again Apache life can be lived with all its exaltations.*

And so Tis-ta-dae and Lozen went to sleep, each thinking of the other, yet refusing to consider any personal life but Apache duty and devotion to Ussen.

As they drifted to sleep they had on their minds the buffalo hunt and the excitement they had each felt when Lozen plucked Tis-ta-dae from beneath the hooves of a stampeding herd. Their dreams carried them back to that exciting summer when Apaches still controlled their own destinies.

CHAPTER NINE

Buffalo Hunt

Late that summer, the entire Warm Springs band, centered around Ojos Caliente, packed up all of their camping gear and set off to the east towards the buffalo plains. The chill of fall was in the air and there had been reports from their relatives, the Mescalero, that the buffalo had come far to the south that year and there were plenty of animals and no sign of Comanches. Lozen was in her late teens and had been on only one other buffalo expedition and that when she was a young girl. She keenly looked forward to the excitement of the hunt and the good fortune it would bring her band to take in a supply of buffalo hides which were highly valued.

There had been a good supply of rain all summer long but the Rio Grande, when they reached it, was at a very low stage because the rains had been evenly measured and had not produced excess runoff. The band numbered two hundred-fifty. Almost everyone in the band took part in the expedition with the exception of some of the older people, the very young, and a few families whose job it was to maintain the summer camps.

Instead of striking out directly for the plains which would have required passing through the Mal Pais, the band pushed towards the sacred mountain called Salinas by the Mexicans and, skirting to the south, took the old trail between the Mal Pais and the white sands towards the Sacramentos. As soon as they crossed the desert they headed almost due east, skirting the northern edge of Sierra Blanca before starting the downhill journey to the plains.

As the band began to leave the mountainous area they met up with a smaller group of Mescaleros who were joining them on the hunt. The combined group was in excess of three hundred fifty strong and presented a formidable party. With such strength they were not as apprehensive of Comanches as they might have otherwise been. When the two Apache groups joined, the young folks sought each other out and were busily renewing friendships as they made their way down the slopes towards the Pecos River.

Lozen joined the young maidens but soon found that all of her old friends were not there. Many had married and were with their own families. Lozen quickly tired of the silly banter the young single women enjoyed. She moved her pony at a trot towards the main body until she came to a large family group she recognized. One of the young wives was a friend of hers from three summers earlier.

Upon seeing her old friend Lozen spoke up, "Autumn Moon, do you recognize me, I'm Lozen."

Autumn Moon knew who her old friend was and smiled broadly, "Of course, Lozen, it has been some time since we played together as young girls."

Lozen smiled wistfully realizing that there had been no insult intended and hastily added, "Yes, that is true, and we will never have the opportunity again because I see you are now a married woman."

Autumn Moon nodded her head energetically and responded, "Yes, Lozen, I have a wonderful husband. He is a great brave and a wonderful provider, and he has given me a son. That is him in front in my mother's arms."

Lozen nudged her horse on the flanks and quickly gained a place alongside Autumn Moon's mother where she could reach over and grasp the young boy and hold him upward as they rode along, admiring his size and strength.

She finally handed the child back. "Here, mother, I do not wish to drop this precious package. I must return him to your strong and safe arms."

The old grandmother received the child lovingly into her arms. As she did, she gave Lozen a broad, grateful, mostly toothless smile which she partially concealed with her free hand.

Lozen fell back alongside of her friend who screwed up the courage to ask, "Why is it that you are still a single girl?"

Lozen emphatically replied, "There is no one that I want. Believe me, there is no one I have met yet that I would defer to in any way. I'm just not interested."

Lozen's friend reacted to the obvious passion her question had roused and said, "I did not intend to pry. I'm sorry. It's none of my business."

Lozen softened her response this time and said, "No, you are perfectly right to ask. I hope that there comes a day when I too will be married like you and have a family but that time has not come and there is much that I feel I must do. No! It's more like I'm obligated to some task before I can enjoy those pleasures. I don't understand it but I know that I must follow Ussen's will."

The two young women continued to visit with each other as the procession wound down towards the plains below and finally camped for the night about ten miles from the Pecos River.

The next morning everyone was up early because they were on the buffalo plains and could encounter their quarry at any moment. The night before, some of the hunters had thought they had spied a few stragglers in the distance but they could not be sure. Excitement was running high as everyone prepared for the hunt. When the warriors presented themselves the following morning for instructions, Lozen, fully armed, rode her pony into the line and awaited her assignment.

She had never been on a hunt as a participant before. In fact, no Apache woman had ever hunted the buffalo before. The men were uneasy, looking at each other as Lozen entered their line. They were wondering how the Chiefs would handle this invasion of their male province. Since Victorio's band was the largest, the Mescaleros acceded to his leadership and asked him to take over control of the hunt. Victorio divided the band into four groups and assigned Lozen to the third group. While there were many of the men who would have preferred that Lozen not be with them, no one dared challenge the leadership of Victorio.

With the assignments made, the four hunting parties rapidly moved out onto the plains in search of their quarry. As a precaution, scouts had been sent to the north and to the south to act as eyes for the group in case there were Comanches in the vicinity, even though Lozen, the night before, had been consulted and had proclaimed that there was no Comanche menace on the plains. The Mescalero were sure that the Comanches had already passed through this country on their way to the autumn raids in Old Mexico.

Within an hour the hunting parties were busily engaged in pursuing their quarry and in no time Lozen had deftly killed her first buffalo, a large bull, with three arrows all planted within the heart. By noon there were a hundred buffalo on the ground and the balance of the tribe had been sent for to begin cutting off the hides and preparing the meat for curing.

Lozen's group had turned back from their quarry as enough buffalo had been killed and were hurrying back to help in the job of securing their kill when they came across a small herd of buffalo coming out of a ravine. The thrill of the hunt was upon the Indians and, with a yell, they charged down on the small band, which wheeled to the right and began a headlong flight. Just then, a group of Apaches climbed out of the ravine directly in the path of the buffalo and instantly took flight ahead of the charging animals.

On one of the ponies a young boy was riding in back of his mother and as she goaded the mount forward he fell off and was standing directly in the path of the charging bison. Lozen had worked her way up to the front of the small rampaging herd when she saw what had happened and, letting go of her weapons, coaxed her horse with a merciless beating of her heels on its flanks to run faster and faster. The boy saw her coming and quickly raised his arms. As Lozen's arms grasped him he held to her so firmly that he almost tore both of them from her mount. The force of the pick up caused her to lurch to the right as the boy's hips banged against the withers of the horse. For a moment, they were each in a precarious position, unbalanced and ready to tumble from the horse under the hooves of the buffalo.

Finally, Lozen, with her great strength, loosened her left hand from the grasp of the boy and was able to grab the horse's mane and pull the youngster up onto her mount in front of her. Within seconds they had outdistanced the buffalo which had veered off on another course. Everyone in both parties marveled at this amazing rescue of an Apache boy whose life surely had been at an end until this brave Apache maiden risked her own life to save him.

With the emergency over, Lozen looked at the boy for the first time. She recognized him immediately as the son of a prominent family in the band. He was Tis-ta-dae. She had noticed him on several occasions and had been greatly impressed by his marvelous athletic abilities.

He was very embarrassed as he stammered his thanks to Lozen, "You are a very brave woman. You have saved my life. I will be forever grateful."

Lozen smiled and replied, "You are a fine warrior. No doubt, some day, you will do just as much for me." They rode together back to where a large group of Apaches had assembled and were busy butchering buffalo.

That night, as the tribe assembled for their evening bivouac, word spread rapidly of the rescue that day and everyone came by to visit with Tis-ta-dae and Lozen and tell them how happy they were that they were both alive. Victorio was particularly proud. He knew there had been some criticism of him for including Lozen in the hunt and he now felt fully vindicated. In visiting that night with a Mescalero sub-Chief, Mushkish, he had to brag on his sister and proudly told his Mescalero colleague that, were she a man, she would indeed be the premier warrior of the Apache Nation. Mushkish and two of his friends, who were listening, nodded their heads with great vigor. There was no doubt about it; the woman would have been like a mountain lion had she been given the body of a man.

"In fact," Mushkish replied, "I think she can hold her own with most of the Apache men I've known."

Victorio was very grateful for this comment as he was proud of his sister but also embarrassed that she was not married and would not even discuss the proposals he presented to her. He volunteered to the Mescalero Chief that he had for many years hoped that Lozen would find a man she liked so that he could arrange a marriage for her but that she refused and was fanatical in her belief that she could not marry until some task that Ussen had prepared her for was completed. This comment provoked a great deal of interest from the Mescaleros as any time there was talk of powers or obligations involving Ussen, there was great interest. This was the business that concerned every Apache. They pressed Victorio for more information.

Victorio replied, "I know not. Only Lozen and my mother have any idea what it is but she has great powers that have been given by Ussen, that is obvious. She is like no other Apache alive when it comes to foretelling danger. We depend on her almost daily."

Mushkish, after hearing all of this, solemnly said to Victorio, "I will be happy to take on another wife if Lozen would care to share the wickiup of a Mescalero."

Victorio grasped his friend by both arms and smiled broadly. "Old friend, you are kind to make that offer. I would like nothing better than to have our families joined in a marriage union but I am sure that Lozen is still on her quest, whatever it might be. But I shall discuss the matter with her."

Later that night Victorio stopped by the campsite of his mother and father where Lozen was helping her mother clean the camp before they retired for the night. He told Lozen that she had received another offer of marriage.

Lozen was shocked that Victorio would bring the matter up in front of their mother but quickly replied, "No, there is no way that I would consider anyone; Warm Springs or Mescalero. Not now. Not now."

Victorio smiled and said, "But you don't know who it is. Don't you want to know? Aren't you interested?"

Lozen replied shyly, "Well, maybe you can tell me who it is. I'm still not interested, but tell me anyway, my brother."

Victorio smiled, happy to know that his sister wasn't that far gone on her notion of a holy mission.

He answered, "Fear not, my sister, it was the best match you could make here today. It was the Mescalero Chief, Mushkish."

Apache Tears

CHAPTER TEN

The Dreamer

For days everyone questioned Lozen for information about relatives and friends. Nana repeatedly grilled her for more information on the Apache messiah Noch-ay-del-Kline. She repeatedly told Nana that the "Dreamer" claimed that his power was the ability to summon the dead and that the dead chiefs were speaking through him, urging the Apaches to rise and force the white-eyes and Mexicans from Apache lands.

Nana was profoundly excited at this news. He confided in Lozen, "I must risk the trip to San Carlos and even risk possible capture by soldiers to see for myself this man of power and learn his vision of the Apache regaining their homeland." Lozen wanted to accompany him but Nana forbade her doing so saying, "I order you to stay behind and guard the band with your power of vision." Lozen had no recourse but to obey as she had been ordered.

Nana was gone for more than a month when Lozen, who had been maintaining a vigil at the head of the zigzag trail in vigil, saw his bent figure laboring up the torturing trail. She hailed him as she neared her viewpoint, "Welcome, great Nantan, I have been waiting here for two weeks to be sure of your return."

Nana gasped for breath after the arduous climb and responded in bursts, "Fear not for me – Little Sister – Ussen himself has propelled me here – with great news for the Apache people."

That night the Chihenne and Netdahe gathered around the coals of the great campfire. After the drums fell silent they heard Nana tell about the miracle he had witnessed through the power of the "Dreamer."

Nana poked a long stick among the embers of the fire and blew softly across the coals bringing a few flames to life. In the flickering light he slowly moved his head, surveying his rapt audience. He began speaking in a soft, reverent tone first offering a prayer to Ussen, addressing his audience, "My Brothers hear me well. We Apaches have but one chance to remain free. If we fail, we all will die or become slaves and servants of the enemy."

Juh interrupted, "Death is a welcome freedom compared to capture and disgrace. Tell us if you saw the dead chiefs and what did they say?"

Nana leaned forward, turning his head to the left and looking into the eyes of Juh. With piercing intensity he said, "Yes! I saw the dead chiefs. The greatest of the Apaches: Cochise, Mangas, our brother Victorio, and the father of all, Mahko. They did not speak, but they showed by sign what we must do."

With the mention of Mahko the excitement of anticipation quickened for everyone there believed himself to be descended from the greatest of all the chiefs.

Nana continued, "When I reached San Carlos there was no one left near the soldier's post but the old, the sick, and the very young, who all complained at having to stay behind. I slipped into the camp nearest the soldiers' tents and was told by Begay, the blind one, that she had begged to be taken along so that the power of the dead chiefs would restore her sight. She begged me to help her up the trail to where the 'Dreamer' was camped." Nana coughed softly and continued, "It was midnight when I left San Carlos and the warmth of dawn was slipping over the ridge when I reached the camp of the 'Dreamer'."

He continued, "When I reached the camp, the place was filled with excitement. I spoke to friends who didn't answer but stared back with blank faces, their minds obviously locked with that of the "Dreamer" in calling on the chiefs to appear. Within minutes after I joined them, the dancers formed a line of two and three abreast and began to climb the trail toward the ridge where, through an early morning mist, the light of dawn was breaking. Noch-ay-del-Kline was at the front, laboring up the trail, obviously drained from a night of dancing and prophesy."

Nana paused, stirred the embers again. He blew a few weak flames to life before continuing. "I was so determined to see what happened that I rudely forced my way up the line of followers until I was just behind the 'Dreamer' when he stopped and fell to his knees, pointing with both arms outstretched to the ridge above saying 'See, there they are. See them. They are with us now and we are with them.'"

A cold sweat had broken out over the body of Nana and he was obviously experiencing distress and loss of control as his emotions welled.

Nana stood up and raised his hands, pointing across the dying embers as he spoke, "The 'Dreamer' said, 'See them. They are here. They are us! We are them!' I looked up and there, rising through the morning mist, I saw for myself the chiefs clothed in a veil of mist. Their bodies were much greater than they had been in life. Yes, much, much greater. Many times greater. They rose ever taller and taller. I saw Cochise, Mangas, and Victorio, side by side, stripped down to the waist, their shirts folded in their belts, their cheeks slashed in red and white paint, prepared for battle." Nana's outstretched arms began to shake and his voice faltered as he continued to speak. "The people around me began to call their dead leaders and then the 'Dreamer' cried, 'Tell us, you who are the best of us, what must we do to remain Apache?'"

Nana raised the pitch of his voice and slowed his delivery as he continued his relation. "Answering the 'Dreamer' a new apparition appeared, it was the great Mahko himself rising in back of the other three as if he were the tip of an arrow. He, too, was stripped to the waist and wore the bronze paint of the Bedonkohe."

Nana's audience was catatonic as they themselves began to conjure the visions of the great chiefs reincarnate and they hung on every word as Nana concluded his story. "With Makho's appearance, the mists began to swirl and the figures were more transparent. Makho raised his right arm with clenched fist and with great power slammed his arm downward as the mists swirled more rapidly and enveloped the chiefs and obscured our view."

His body shaking with emotion, Nana lowered his arms and sat down on a pine log while the audience peered into the night sky where Nana had pointed, hoping that the chiefs would appear to them as well.

Nana had sat down next to Lozen who stood up. She placed her hands on his shoulders asked, "Tell us, dear Nantan, what does it mean?"

Nana was emotionally drained but before he could raise his head and speak, Juh interjected, "It means we must fight. The closed fist of Makho is the strength of the Apache. The blow downward is how we use this strength. The chiefs are telling us that there is no point in trying to negotiate with the Mexicans or the Americans. There we found nothing but treachery and deceit. They want our land. They want to bend us to their ways. They want our lives. We must fight."

Nana nodded his head in assent and, standing again, said, "Juh is right. The time has come for us to avenge our dead. Tomorrow, the Chihenne will prepare for the final battle."

CHAPTER ELEVEN

Vengeance

For two weeks after Nana recounted the miraculous summoning of the dead Chiefs, the Chihenne pulled together their forces. Every family visited a cache where they had laid up ammunition, food, and hides and made sure that each warrior would leave camp with the best equipment possible. Ammunition was the most valued component of the warrior's supplies, along with dried meat, mesquite cakes, and water bags.

When the preparations were complete, Nana set the time for the vengeance dance to trigger the expedition. On the appointed night, the moon was full and in the shimmering light of the great fire, everyone clearly saw the four warriors approaching from the east to call upon their companions to display their zeal and devotion to the coming raid.

A skin had been stretched over the great drum and tied down to keep it taut. For an hour before the dancers appeared the other Chihenne were gathered to the west of the fire around the great drum, listening to its mournful peal and the increasing emotion of the chanters. It was most unusual for a woman to join in such a chorus but no one was surprised when Lozen did just that, raising her voice in unison with them.

Lozen, for days, had begged Nana to include her in his battle plan but he had spurned her entreaties, wanting her to stay in camp and protect the sanctuary with her power. He had, however, that day, succumbed to her entreaty when she spoke to him using his Chihenne name, "Kas Taiden, I have asked for little and followed your every command. I beg you to look in your heart and let me be part of this blow you are going to strike to start us on the path back to freedom and to avenge the death of my brother, Beduiat."

Nana was struck with Lozen's lapse back to his Apache name and that of Victorio which was rarely used. The Apaches had adopted their chief's common name in everyday use and only resorted to their birth names when a situation was grave. Nana instantly responded to Lozen's ploy, "Little Sister, you have called my name. No Apache can refuse another Apache where there is such an appeal. You may come along. In fact, since you insist, I am going to entrust you with the most important mission that anyone in this war can have."

Lozen's smile could not be suppressed. It was born from the release of the strong passion that compelled her to insist on her inclusion. She put her hand on Nana's shoulder and said, "Give me any duty. I will not fail."

Nana, now himself smiling, realized that Lozen's guile had procured his assent. He put his right hand over her palm and then embraced her, saying, "You will leave at first light and alone travel the desert to where the great river enters the canyon and there strike north for the Mescalero. Tell them I am coming and that I want every Chihenne to meet me in one week at the canyon called Alamo. Tell the Mescalero warriors that they are welcome to join in this holy mission."

When the dancers neared the fire they began to circle, first to the north, then the other cardinal directions, and called on their brothers by name, "Tis-ta-dae," called the lead dancer, "Come and join us, we need your strong arm and unerring eye."

"Baishan," called another, "This is your dance. Your family has been killed by the enemy. Come help us pay them back."

And on it went, each warrior summoned jumping up and joining the wheeling dancers.

The fire cast an eerie glow on the impassioned figures as they, with increasing abandon, leaped and jumped accompanied by the crackling piñon and pitch knots blazing in the fire. As the fire flamed, so did the passions of the dancers and their audience. One by one the warriors joined the dancers. Shots ringing out in the night heightened the mounting frenzy. The dancers, as they circled in abandon, acted out in pantomime how they would excel in the coming contest and slay the enemy. The viewing participants responded energetically with victory screams and by shooting their rifles into the air.

Lozen would have joined the dancers, but even she, given all the license she had enjoyed in the past, didn't challenge this bastion of manhood. She did, however, lustily sing and call out to the dancing warriors, urging on their frenzy.

Shots continued ringing out, now from everyone's guns. Even as short as the ammunition supply was, it was essential that everyone proclaim his zeal and determination to be the best that an Apache warrior could be in a raid that had been demanded by the Great Chiefs. On the dancers wheeled through the night, ignoring fatigue. It was almost dawn before they began to fall out one by one, exhausted physically and drained emotionally.

Nana did not join in the dancing; reserving his strength to force his pain-racked and crippled body through the ordeal he knew lay ahead. Lozen stayed beside him as he beat on the great drum which sent its crescendo reverberating across the canyons and down the mountainside.

With the coming of dawn, the throb of the drum ceased and the Chihenne retreated to their beds for blessed sleep.

Dawn's rosey light saw Lozen depart on a mule that was the best one in the Apache camp. Nana wanted her to be well mounted on a dependable animal and insisted that she take the mule that would otherwise have been his. Its name was Chubasco. He stood a full 16 hands and was a dark roan color with a black mane that narrowed to a strip down his back ending in a free flowing tail. Before she left camp in advance of the war party, Nana counseled her, "Avoid all contact and let nothing stop you from reaching the Ruidoso to gather the strength we need to punish our enemies so that they will leave this country rather than continue to risk the might of our fists."

Lozen was surprised that she was leaving on her mission before Juh had returned from Casas Grandes with the other Netdahe warriors. Nana, however, had concluded that Juh was on a drunk and could not be depended upon at this time. He was determined to take his revenge with only the Chihenne in the war party.

Lozen had dressed as a Mexican peasant and not as an Apache. She was to pose as a domestic from a Mexican ranch; one who had been raised by the whites after being captured as a child. Her story was that she was on her way to El Paso for medical supplies. She even carried a note written by a Mexican captive who had converted to the Netdahe. The note called on a merchant to supply her with iodine, sulphur, and cacao. Lozen didn't need the note, crossing the desert floor without incident.

After crossing the El Paso/Chihuahua Road, she turned northward toward Fort Quitman where she crossed the Rio Grande. Her heart was heavy when she passed the place where only a year earlier the tribe had turned back toward Mexico to be destroyed at Tres Castillas. Having crossed the Rio Grande she sought shelter in a cave where food had been cached and, before falling asleep, looked to the south toward Tres Castillas, just two days ride away. Her heart was heavy as she recalled the death of Victorio and so many others of her family. With her hands raised in supplication over an altar fire, she spoke aloud, "Ussen. Give me the power to protect Kas Taiden and the Chihenne. I was not able to warn Victorio when he reached Tres Castillas. Please, Ussen, keep my power alive and let me be with my people when they need me. I am not good for anything else. I have not married or even known a man. Show me; please show me, that I am doing what you want. Give me a sign that I am doing your will."

The night sky was still and the only response to Lozen's passionate entreaty was the rustling of twigs as a pack rat, sharing the cave with her, started out on his nightly round of food gathering.

The waning moon was still bright when Lozen unpicketed her mule before dawn and struck out for the Mescalero Reservation. As she rode up the canyon, she mused on her inability to understand what is was that Ussen had demanded of her. She thought to herself, *I failed completely at Tres Castillas. I wonder if I really have a power because, when my people needed it most, I was not even there. What has been the purpose of my life, why do I constantly have these recurring doubts about my role? Why is it that sometimes I can call on the future and other times I can't? Am I really different from the other Apaches, or is it just my imagination? Why am I not with Victorio now or dead with the other Chihenne? Is there some purpose in my going on? Please, Ussen send me a sign.*

Lozen heightened her senses hoping for a response or sign but was met with silence.

Apache Tears

CHAPTER TWELVE

Fire with Fire

She rode briskly up the dry canyon bottom which headed north and, by early morning, she had reached the flats that stretch out towards the salt lakes at the foot of the Guadalupe Mountains. Lozen scanned the mountains looking for the telltale plume of dust that a cavalry patrol would raise. Seeing none, she spoke softly to her mule, "Chubasco. Show me why Nana is so proud of you. Carry me across this open country where not even an Apache can hide as if you had the wings of an eagle."

As she spoke, she contracted her knees and commanded Chubasco to pick up the gait. The mule quickened his pace and bore Lozen with seemingly effortless ease toward the distant crag of Signal Peak. Off to the right Lozen could see a flock of buzzards wheeling in a thermal while up ahead a single eagle patrolled lazily.

Halfway across the desert floor she surprised a small band of Big Horn sheep that had been sheltering from the sun in the cover of a mesquite tree growing in a small arroyo. A little further along Lozen's passage galvanized a small herd of pronghorns to race off towards the looming Guadalupes.

Lozen seized the opportunity to let her mount compete in the race by digging her heels into both flanks and calling out, "Fly like the wind, Chubasco. Show these whirlwinds of the desert what a mule of Apache blood can do."

Chubasco responded, his ears at a peak and his nostrils flaring. This was a welcome relief to the monotony of the slow travel gait and off he raced, with Lozen low on his back, shouting in his ear, "Run, Chubasco, run. Run as if every Buffalo Soldier in Apacheria is at your heels."

The mule responded willingly to Lozen's exhortation, and forced the antelope to take the challenge seriously by picking up their pace, racing faster and faster. The chase was exciting after the tedious days of boredom but Lozen, as quickly as she had urged her mount on, pulled him back. Calling, "Stop, now. Stop, my brave whirlwind, that is enough. If there are soldiers anywhere near, they will think that Victorio and all of the Chihenne have returned from the dead when they see the billows of desert dust we send into the sky."

The mule had run so well that Lozen's confidence was bolstered and she leaned over and spoke into his ear, "How can they catch you? We'll just throw caution away and race like the wind into the mountain sanctuary ahead."

The mule settled back into his easy gait, happy to be ridden by a master whose body accommodated his undulating muscles and bonded to him like a tight fitting glove. The rest of the trip over the desert floor to the salt lake was placid with only a jackrabbit or two in view. When Chubasco and Lozen reached the brow of the flats, after passing the ruins of the old Butterfield Stage station on the edge of the salt lake, they dropped down to the saline lagoon with its crusted salt formations. Lozen paused and debated whether to skirt to the left or right. There were easy trails in both directions but there was also danger of being ambushed by a charging cavalry patrol as the escarpment of the Guadalupe Mountains was almost inaccessible at this point. Moving to the west, however, left her no sanctuary at all. So she cast discretion aside and, as the receding shorelines were obviously much reduced from drought, she plunged straight ahead through the basin itself, confident that her strong and heroic companion would carry her through any deep water or marshy quicksand. Her decision proved wise and Lozen was soon through the salt deposits and back into the hummocks and arroyos of the desert floor which soon gave way to the foothills of the Sacramento Mountains.

As she gained altitude, she began to see the old mescal pits scattered about along with campsites in great number. She was soon in the mountains themselves. She skirted east of Alamo Canyon and reached the narrow mountain valley where the Mescalero agency office was located.

She turned up a side canyon and found shelter in a dense stand of piñons. There she tied her mule to a tree and spent the rest of the daylight gathering browse and forage for Chubasco. She couldn't leave him hobbled as there were certain to be Buffalo Soldiers near the agency, and they might be curious about a strange mule in their midst.

When night came Lozen left the grove and made her way further up the side canyon to a group of log cabins she had not seen before. A Mescalero who had been with Juh in Mexico had given her directions to this spot. He had told her that there were marriage ties with a Chihenne in this particular camp.

After securing her mount Lozen slipped through a pine thicket to the clearing where she expected to find her kinsmen. She cautiously approached the nearest log cabin in a group of five. Upon reaching the door, she softly called out, "Delshi, are you there? It is your cousin, Lozen."

There was no immediate response so Lozen raised her voice and called again while knocking at the door. A timid response accompanied her knock. "Lozen. It is you?"

Lozen's reply was to pull the latchstring and enter the candlelit room. Her cousin, Delshi, rushed to embrace her, "Lozen, it is a miracle. We had feared that you were dead. How wonderful to see you."

The two women were ebullient in their embrace, eager to trade news of their family and friends.

The news that shocked Lozen was that there was a troop of cavalry camped not three miles away at the Agency's office. Camped alongside them, unbelievingly, was a squad of Chiricahua scouts, led by Chief Eugene Chihuahua. The Warm Springs had dealt with Pueblo scouts from Ysleta and even Apache scouts from San Carlos but never their fellow Southern Apache. As Lozen was appreciating the enormity of this news, Delshi's husband entered the room. Lozen quickly told him why she had sought them out, "I am here to recruit Warm Springs and Mescaleros to join Nana on a vengeance raid to atone for the death of Victorio and convince the whites they must leave our lands." She recounted Nana's experience with The Dreamer and the call of the old Chiefs to expel everyone from Indian lands.

Lozen passionately called on her kinsmen to join the venerable Nana in convincing the Americans that holding Apache land required a higher price than they would pay. All agreed that the presence of cavalry troops, with support from Chiracahuas, required urgent recruiting and an early departure to join Nana at the rendezvous at Alamo Canyon.

The three spread out, quickly seeking volunteers to join Nana. By midnight more than thirty excited warriors, jaded by the monotony of the reservation, had gathered in Delshi's house. They were a mixed group of Warm Springs men who had Mescalero wives and Mescalero men anxious to fight alongside the legendary Nana.

The group slipped quietly from the reservation. By dawn's light they dropped into Alamo Canyon where Nana was waiting for Lozen's appearance and the much needed reinforcements.

Nana had reached Alamo Canyon near dusk the day before. On the way, he had surprised a packtrain of suppliers carrying rations to the Buffalo Soldiers. Two packers were dead and a third had been wounded but had successfully fled the scene. Lozen's news was startling. It galvanized Nana to immediately break camp and order his augmented force to leave the canyon and dash across the desert floor towards the San Andreas range looming through a haze of humidity across the desert.

As they rushed toward the desert floor Lozen rudely asked Nana why there were only 15 warriors in Nana's party. "Where are the Nedeheshe?" she pressed. Nana, in disgust, explained, "Juh went to Janos with most of his warriors. They all got drunk."

Nana continued in gasps as they loped along side by side, "They were straggling back as we were leaving, a few at a time. I told them to stay behind. I told them they were not worthy to avenge the death of Victorio."

Lozen agreed and commented woefully, "We will be the end of ourselves."

As the band paced itself across the sands heading toward Laguna Spring, they were being trailed, not two hours behind, by Sergeant Chihuahua and his scouts who, in turn, were ahead of Lieutenant Guilfoille's troop of cavalry. Nana had seen their dust rising in the still air and realized that they could not tarry long for water. On reaching the springs they found three Mexicans there who were promptly shot and scavenged for ammunition. As soon as their canteens were filled and the horses watered Nana ordered all to press towards the San Andreas which were now casting their shade towards them.

When Nana's band reached the eastern escarpment of the San Andreas, they rested their mounts and looked back across the desert floor. The progress of the troops was clearly disclosed by the plume of dust and, out ahead of it, the smaller dust signal of Sergeant Chihuahua and the Chiricahua scouts.

Nana, after gazing at the sign of the pursuers, turned to Lozen and instructed her to scout the Rio Grande valley, "Cross the San Andreas at the old trail and see if there are soldiers in the valley of the Rio Bravo."

Lozen protested, preferring to stay with the expedition. "Please, Nantan, let me stay with you where I can better serve our cause."

Nana replied, "You can best serve the Chihenne by being our eyes and giving us warning of the enemy," pausing, "Go now, swiftly. We will stay on this side of the mountains and meet you in four days at the cave of Cuchillo Negro."

Lozen submitted to her mentor and, as the war party moved out, she struck westward towards the old trial.

Four hours later when Chihuahua reached the branching trail of Lozen, he halted the scouts and confided to the Chief of Scouts, Bennett, in passable English. "Nana sends warrior to search the river for soldiers. He moves north to wait for the warrior to give him news."

Bennett readily agreed, "You stay on their trail. Try to hold them up. I am going back to hurry up the soldiers."

Chihuahua wasted no time in urging the scouts northward. Bennett sped back towards Guilfoille's troop. While Bennett back-tracked towards the cavalry, Lozen worked across the rocky trail over the San Andreas. As she reached the top, a burgeoning mushroom of black clouds cut loose their moisture and washed the parched land. Lozen, still mounted on Chubasco, enjoyed the cold embrace of the downpour, even welcoming the sting of some hail within the storm. The same storm moving northwards erased the trail of the war party, but with Chihuahua thinking where he would be headed himself, the scouts pressed on towards the cave of Cuchillo Negro. He was thinking to himself that it was not five years ago that he and Nana had camped at that cave and admired its defenses.

While Apache chased Apache, Lozen, in her Mexican garb, scoured the Rio Grande valley, studying the sign of every trail while avoiding the scattered farms and settlements. At the end of three days of reconnoitering it was obvious that the signs she had seen were entirely local and that no large group of horsemen was active in the valley. She also felt good about the absence of danger and began to worry about Nana and the warriors with their own wily brethren on their trail.

Full of apprehension, she turned back to the east after crossing the river and rode up a precipitous and jagged trail that meandered through the Fray Christobal Range. As she neared the summit, she stopped to rest. A premonition of company was quickly confirmed by a rattling of stone being dislodged by a pony being driven ahead of the descending troop of Apache raiders. Lozen remained concealed until she was sure it was Nana.

When the first warrior came into view, she rushed to join her kinsman. Nana was close to the lead. Without stopping, he signaled Lozen to fall in beside him. There was an hour of light left and Nana wanted to be out of the barrancas of the foothills while there was still light. As they moved along, Nana received Lozen's report and was gratified. He complemented her thoroughness, "Little Sister, again you make me proud. In the morning we will strike across the valley and reach the sanctuary of the San Mateos."

Lozen nodded and queried Nana, "I see that you have wounded with you. What has happened?"

Nana recounted the surprise they had suffered as a result of Chihuahua's expertise and related a sharp battle at the cave of Cuchillo Negro in Mockingbird Gap. They had lost two horses, several mules, and all of their provisions. Two warriors had been hit. Nana, gasping from the pounding he was taking as the horse hurried down the trail, continued, "Two of the Mescaleros have been wounded, one badly. I will need your help dressing their wounds."

Lozen nodded her assent as the two rushed on, leading the party to the valley floor. Once out of the jagged rocks, they made a cold camp as the twilight faded and, by the dim moonlight, attended the wounded men.

While Lozen did her best to dress the wound of the warrior with the less serious injury, Nana was working to save the life of the Mescalero who had been badly hit in the thigh. He stuffed the wound with dried grass and bandaged it tight with his own tunic but to no avail. The wound continued to hemorrhage badly. The rough flight from the San Andreas had been too much for the brave man. The Mescalero lasted another hour and then died, quietly. Before midnight, his body was stuffed into a crevice and rocks were hastily placed on top of him. Having seen to their dead companion the party immediately left for the sanctuary of the San Mateos.

Apache Tears

CHAPTER THIRTEEN

Hide and Seek

The next morning Nana had everyone awake at first light. He quickly called in the posted guards and the two Apaches who had maintained a false camp through the night. He outlined a plan to them to steal livestock and supplies in the Rio Grande valley. Lozen would be sent ahead to scout for cavalry in the San Mateos whose precipitous vastness Nana would next penetrate.

Lozen did not argue about her assignment. She knew that Nana was giving her a task as important as any and she set out on Chubasco whose endurance was becoming legendary. She pushed deep into the San Mateos which rise majestically from the desert floor, cut by deep canyons filled with rock and mountain debris, impenetrable to all except the most gifted and determined adventurers.

Lozen, for two days, cut across the canyons seeking vantage points from which she could scour the San Mateos Range and Rio Grande valley for signs of cavalry. Her destination was a promontory overlooking Red Canyon that had an excellent view of Fort Craig in the valley floor. It was at Fort Craig that Nana had predicted Colonel Hatch would be mounting a campaign against the hostiles. The wily Nana had decided that striking north into the heart of the cavalry strength would be the area least patrolled and easiest to penetrate in a daring plan to carry his raid into northern New Mexico to the Navajo Reservation where he hoped to lure further recruits into his campaign. He was convinced that his bold move might cause the Americans to abandon the Gila and retreat to the foreign lands from whence they came.

Lozen saw only the barest signs of activity below her with no telltale dust of troop movements. She was about to leave her post and report back to Nana when a sensation of excitement raced through her body. She intently turned to the north and looked almost straight down, her eyes drown as if by a magnet, and there below her, raising no dust because of the rocky footing, was a large party of miners and Mexican farmers pushing up Red Canyon. She spoke softly to Chubasco standing beside her, gently caressing him with her hand, "Look, Chubasco! They are following your trail up the canyon floor. What fools to be in the bottom if they think that Chihenne are at hand."

She led her mount back from the summit. Once shielded by the terrain she hurried down the adjoining canyon until she hit a place where the foothills permitted her to cut across and reach Nana who had planned their rendezvous two miles south of where the party was proceeding up Red Canyon.

When Lozen reached Nana, he excitedly told her that they had killed two Mexican farmers at Cuchillo Creek and two miners and six sheepherders near the stage stop at Cantarecio. As a result, he and his warriors were on fresh mounts. Lozen waited politely until Nana finished describing the Chihenne retribution. She then, excitedly, burst in, "Nana, there are at least forty whites and Mexicans in the deep canyon that leads to Fort Craig. They have been following the tracks of Chubasco and are now resting and eating."

Nana's face erupted into a grim smile as he queried, "Horses and mules? Are there many?"

Lozen shot back, "They're all well mounted and have a remuda as well."

Nana disposed his forces with one-half coming in above and one-half below the site Lozen had described as the rock ledge where the party was camped. Nana, with Lozen beside him, quietly positioned himself directly south of the expeditionary force. The men below were finishing their noon meal and beginning to take a siesta with only two guards posted alongside the picketed horses. Nana watched while his men took their posts. Seeing them in place, he signaled with his carbine to stampede the stock down the canyon and he himself fired the first shot into the unwary posse. The canyon reverberated with rifle fire as the Apaches, from their vantage points, poured a merciless fire down on the scattering men.

Nana could see that one of the horse guards was down and motionless and the other, limping badly, was dashing from rock to rock trying to rejoin his companions who were being cut down by crossfire. The force had picked a beautiful place to camp at a bubbling spring but there was precious little cover to protect them from Apache marksmen. Every rock had two or three men beside it trying to find a shielded side.

Nana saw his men cut the picket ropes and wave their blankets to spook the herd of livestock down the canyon. Wisely, he shouted to his men to break off the engagement and he and Lozen kept firing from their vantage point high above the hapless would-be pursuers. Once every Apache had successfully abandoned the canyon and headed for the rendezvous, Nana and Lozen left and followed suit.

When Nana and Lozen stopped their punishing fire of interdiction, they joined the others and celebrated their good fortune. They had acquired an additional 50 head of stock. Everyone was well mounted, there was a good remuda of replacements, and a commissary on the hoof.

Nana was elated and announced that they would roast a mule to celebrate their good fortune. Lozen was as hungry as the rest of the Apaches, but panicked when Nana decided that Chubasco would be the feast. Chubasco had gone lame while crossing a rockslide to reach the rendezvous.

Lozen begged Nana for the life of her companion, "Oh Great Chief, spare me this mule. He has served me well and is as much a Chihenne as I."

Nana sternly replied, "We are a raiding party. There is no room for sentiment and emotion. Every Apache must sacrifice for the common good."

Lozen pressed her case and, dropping on one knee, held her hands up in supplication, pleading, "Nana. Please. Just this once. Just for me."

The taciturn leader turned his back so that Lozen would not see the smile he couldn't suppress, so struck was he by the entreaty of his charge to spare the mule who had given her such service. "Very well," he stammered. "Let him go. Cut him free. If this is the reward you want, it is yours."

Lozen threw her arms around Nana's shoulders; almost bringing the old man to the ground, so emotional was she in her embrace. "Thank you, good Nana. I will be the first among the Chihenne to die at your command."

Nana pushed her aside as he staggered upright. He turned and watched Lozen race to where Chubasco was hobbled with the rest of their mounts, quietly feeding. Lozen cut the mule loose and, stretching up, hugged his neck as firmly as she had Nana's and commanded in his lowered ear, "Fly my faithful whirl-wind friend. Leave here at once before you fill these Apache stomachs."

Lozen slapped Chubasco strongly on the rump and pelted him with small rocks to force him down the canyon. The mule was firmly attached to Lozen but stinging missiles convinced him to find greener pastures. He broke into an ungainly trot with his left front foot painfully churning the sands of the dry wash.

The Apache's dined well that night on a less fortunate mount and slept peacefully with sentries both above and below their encampment high on a ridge with a single brave tending a fire at the false camp in the bottom. They felt secure. Lozen had summoned the future and detected no threats and the scouts had reported that the would-be adventurers were limping out onto the plains, carrying their wounded and firing at any movement in the brush as they struggled to reach Fort Craig. These lucky men would have something to tell their grandchildren but only because Nana wanted their mounts and not their lives.

At Fort Craig, an aroused Colonel Hatch was at that moment speculating where Nana might be and railing at his officers for letting the Apaches through. The telegraph lines were burning up with demands for the War Office to stop the Apache scourge. Civilians in every village and hamlet saw an Apache behind every rock. Stories of atrocities and ambush were spreading like wildfire. Even in Victorio's heyday, the frontier had never been so kindled with fires of fear. Nana was extracting a price for the death of Victorio. It didn't matter that the death toll was mounting on U.S. soil, instead of Mexico's. The struggle was Apaches against all intruders. The death of any enemy diminished their number and gave hope for Apache survival.

The day after the capture of the remuda in Red Canyon, Nana's party was camped at Monica Springs in a deep canyon at the north end of the San Mateos Mountains. He had posted Lozen and another warrior as lookouts atop a high outcropping a mile below the site of the springs. In late afternoon Lozen saw the flash of sunlight on army carbines and saw, threading their way through the canyon, a strong detachment of cavalry. Lozen and her companion quickly scrambled down from the outcropping and reached the resting party at Monica Springs with the news that they were being closely pursued. Nana ordered the camp to break and posted four warriors behind high rocks to delay the trailing cavalry.

When the troopers reached Monica Springs, the rear guard opened fire, pinning the cavalry down for an hour while the main party made its way back into the recesses of the rugged San Mateos. As a sudden summer squall erupted over the canyon obscuring vision and pelting man and beast with hail, the warriors beat a retreat from the scene of engagement, leaving the cavalry alone to wonder where the wily Apache would strike next.

Strike they did seven days later, north of the San Mateos when they swept out of the mountains onto the town of Garcia, killing six men and capturing well over a hundred horses to replace the jaded stock they had been riding.

After the battle of Garcia Nana confided in Lozen, "We are going to turn to the northwest to the Navajo Reservation. There we will inflame the Navajos and recruit other members for our war party."

Two days later they were at the village of Seboyeta where two more farmers were surprised and killed in a field and a young girl captured. After a brief skirmish Nana called the band together and announced that they were going to head south, back to the Blue Mountains. Many of the braves protested. Their recent string of successes had excited them and had given them optimism that their adventure was succeeding in pushing the Whites out of the Southwest.

Nana counseled the assembled warriors, pointing out, "The railroad tracks we crossed between here and Garcia were not there a year ago, it is obvious that the Americans have continued to enlarge their presence. With their trains carrying soldiers we are going to be cut off if we attempt to reach the Navajos. There is no point now in going further to the north. We will be very exposed even if the Navajos rise up in arms to the last man, woman, and child to take on our cause."

The lively debate continued between those who respected Nana's wisdom and others who thrived on the exhilaration of dealing their enemies a blow. Nana did not waiver and gave the order to turn south and head for the Mexican border three hundred miles away.

After turning south, Nana instructed Lozen to scout the Rio Grande garrisons to determine where the cavalry units were operating so that they could plan their escape route. Lozen was happy to be off on her own again as she enjoyed the freedom of making her own decisions, being unfettered with the routine of moving a large group. She headed south, crossed the Rio Salado, and passed on the west side of the San Mateos. It took her twenty-four hours to reach Ojos Caliente. She found it, for the moment, deserted although it was still occasionally used as an outpost for Fort Craig.

There was an awesome silence at the springs and Lozen had a terrible premonition of the future when she saw what had once been the bustling campsite of her youth, totally deserted. The abandoned fort and the eroding ruins of the Pueblos who had preceded the Apaches at this garden spot created an aura of foreboding. Lozen tarried long enough to go to the main spring where she drank and recalled her passage to womanhood. A hundred yards above the spring was the campsite where she had rushed to tell her mother the news of her transformation.

Lozen, with heavy heart grieving for her mother and father and all the other members of her family who had died at the hands of the Mexicans and Americans, slipped up the glade above the spring to where the camp had been. All remnants were gone except a few rings of boulders where campfires had once been tended. Sadly, she recalled the wonderful days of her youth and the tragedy into which the tribe had been plunged by the white man's greed for the Apache homeland. She left the scene of her youth and rode through the box down Cañada Alamosa approaching the town of Alamosa lying below the face of the San Mateos range.

She arrived at the village, waited till night, and discerned the campfires of a troop of cavalry camped nearby. As she crept closer to determine the strength of the contingency, she slipped through the picket line of horses and there, to her amazement, she saw in the moonlight, her companion Chubasco. The discovery of her friend diverted Lozen for a moment as she crawled on her stomach to a large rock from where she estimated the strength of the camp at approximately twenty men. Silently, she retraced her steps and cut the thong that held Chubasco to the picket line. Holding her hand over his nose to contain any bray of welcome, she deftly ran her free hand down his leg to check for swelling. Satisfied by what she discerned, she slipped through the chaparral and Apache broom to the mount she had left tethered, Chubasco following of his own accord. She cut her mount loose so that he could follow or stay as he chose and mounted Chubasco. Reunited, they headed back up the Canada to warn Nana of the presence of cavalry. Chubasco's injured leg was fully recovered.

Riding up the canyon she leaned forward and purred in the mule's left ear, "Well, old friend, we're together again. They'll have to eat me before they think of feasting on you, so don't go lame again."

Lozen found Nana on the flat between Canada Alamosa and Cuchillo Negro and warned him of the presence of cavalry further towards the Rio Grande. With the news, Nana promptly turned south and stopped only long enough to attack a farm house, killing all of the occupants, missing the farmer who was in a nearby field when he heard the war whoops of the attacking Apache and took cover.

On reaching the Cuchillo Negro Canyon, Nana turned west to the foothills of the Cuchillo range. He was hampered by the large remuda, pack animals, and booty the party had collected at Garcia and Cebollita. When they reached a little line of hills covered with mesquite and greasewood, Nana stopped and set up defenses on three knolls as the cavalry was fast gaining upon them. Sending the rest of the party ahead, Nana and ten braves stayed behind and fought a rear action battle with the troopers whose strength had been swelled by Mexican ranchers and farmers who knew of Nana's latest attack.

A sharp engagement followed before the Apaches broke and retreated to higher ground. Nana could see that the main force was still laboring up the foothills trying to reach the safety of the more difficult terrain where the troopers would have a hard time following. Again he exhorted the warriors to punish the attacking force.

In the heat of the engagement, ten more warriors joined Nana having been sent by Lozen who was in charge of the retreat of the main body. Nana was vexed that Lozen had exposed the trophies of war by diluting the retreating party but welcomed the addition of new arms. He mounted a counterattack which sent the soldiers back in disarray. The action continued for more than two hours when Nana realized that some of the soldiers and townspeople were flanking him to the left.

He felt that adequate time had been given to the main party to escape and broke off the engagement. Carrying two wounded braves with him, he attempted to pin down the flanking force. Nana then saw another troop of cavalry entering the fray, working their way up a large hill which commanded the field of battle. Leaving three warriors to entertain the flanking force, he reached the summit of the hill before the cavalry did and drove them back with a merciless fire.

Leaving four men behind to cover their retreat, Nana left the field of battle and hastened to join the main party. While there had been no soldiers or farmers killed by the Apaches, there was a severe loss of mounts and many wounded men. The Americans had been dealt a smart defeat.

The pressure on Nana's force intensified the following day when they were challenged by two troops whom they encountered coming up the valley in which the Cuchillo Negro flowed. A typical battle followed with no losses other than livestock on either side. The Apaches retreated into the Black Range towards the headwaters of Alamosa Creek. The Apaches stayed on the west side of the Black Range traversing some of the most difficult terrain in the Southwest, cutting across the grain of the canyons and ridges. Almost half their livestock was lost or became lame during a fifty-mile trek to the south end of the Range where, once again, they crossed over to the east side and rampaged through the mining town of Gold Dust.

After attacking two ranches and gathering up as much stray livestock as they could to replace the animals lost in the traverse of the Black Range, the Apache force headed up the wagon road leading to the Mimbres River via Gavalon Canyon. As the Apaches moved up the canyon, they were followed by a cavalry contingent and an excited mob of citizens from Lake Valley and Hillsboro who made the mistake of pressing the Apaches too hard.

Nana's scouts had warned him of the force coming on their heels. At a narrow, rocky passage Nana set his trap. Wary, the cavalry hesitated to enter the narrows and sent scouts ahead to determine whether or not there was, indeed, an ambush set for them. The excited miners and townspeople, however, rushed up the gorge to display their bravery. When the small force was securely in the encroaching rock ledges, the Apaches loosed a volley which sobered the drunken pursuers many of whom were wounded.

One was left dead and the horses bolted both up and down the canyon. Three troopers trying to reach the trapped miners were themselves cut down while other troopers were hit and wounded. With the lieutenant in charge of the troop dead, one of the sergeants, a Buffalo Soldier, took charge and extricated the living, abandoning all of the horses, ammunition, and other supplies to the Apache.

By mid-afternoon reinforcements from Lake Valley were arriving and the cavalry was again cautiously approaching Gavalon Canyon. Nana, with his booty deep in the mountain fastness, did not resist their advance. The troops were moving very slowly with extreme trepidation and the Apaches escaped without a drop of blood being drawn.

Three days after the battle of Gavalon Canyon, Nana's forces hid out in the desert twenty miles from Fort Cummings where Colonel Hatch, having shifted his command, was pondering his next moves. Lozen had again been sent ahead to scout this disposition of troops. When she reported to Nana that the last detachment had ended their sweep of the country leading south into old Mexico and had retired to Fort Cummings, Nana moved out, passing within an hour's ride of the perplexed and bleeding Colonel Hatch who couldn't understand how a handful of Indians were outwitting West Point's pride and joy, the U.S. Cavalry.

After skirting Fort Cummings, Nana instructed Tis-ta-dae to leave the main group and make a faint to the east. Nana confided to Tis-ta-dae and Lozen, "I want Colonel Hatch to divide his command and resources. Take the Mescaleros with you. They want to see their families."

Tis-ta-dae readily accepted command responsibility and responded to Nana, "You are right and the smaller groups can move faster."

After the two groups parted Nana threw caution to the wind and riding their mounts until they dropped, the Apaches swept toward the Border with little organization or direction. It was almost every man for himself. With the extra mounts, when one horse faltered a brave would take one of the spare horses and continue the all-out pace. Riding night and day they reached the border and rested before proceeding on to the stronghold where they had been but thirty days before, prior to starting their bloody revenge rampage through New Mexico.

Apache Tears

CHAPTER FOURTEEN

The Chili War

After leaving Nana, Tis-ta-dae and his group headed across the Organ Pass. There the Mescaleros who had been in Nana's raid separated and, staying south of the white sands, struck out for their reservation. Tis-ta-dae and the remaining Apaches reached Hueco Tanks at dusk. They quickly reconnoitered the tanks and concluded that there was no one there and settled down for the night while two of the warriors were sent to El Paso to check on the disposition of troops.

Hueco Tanks is a massive granite extrusion that fractured as it cooled. It is a jumble of fissured rocks and boulders of every size, laced with caves formed by volcanic gases. It contains natural depressions that frequently hold water yearlong.

When the Apaches arrived and made their search to see if anyone was present they had examined the accessible caves because they knew that the Pueblo Indians at Ysleta frequently camped at this sacred place, Hueco Tanks. They found no one and there was no evidence of recent camping activities. It would have been unusual to find Pueblos camped there as it was generally used as a summer retreat.

What Tis-ta-dae and the others did not know was that an old Tigua Indian named Shimitigua was camped at Hueco Tanks. He had been there for almost two weeks undergoing a spiritual absolution. He had not picked one of the accessible caves for his camping spot but instead had selected a cave high on the side of a cliff which could only be reached by cautious use of hand and foot holds in a large crevice in the rocks.

Shimitigua had started to make his campfire for the night when he looked to the north and saw the approaching Apaches. He quickly doused the beginning flames of the fire and watched their approach. He knew they were searching for Pueblos as they went from cave to cave and was certain they would find his hiding place. He was lucky that they did not make an effort to reach his shelter although you could see the opening of the cave from the ground. This lack of attention by the Apaches saved his life.

Shimitigua watched the Apaches make camp in a cave in a rock formation directly opposite his. It was a favorite camping spot of travelers because of a large pool of water which was usually present. An extensive cave was adjacent which provided warmth on cold evenings. Shimitigua watched Tis-ta-dae send the two braves to El Paso to scout the military situation.

When the Apaches reached Hueco Tanks Tis-ta-dae asked Lozen, "Do you think it is safe to spend the night here?"

She replied, "For some reason, I am not at ease, but I do not know why. If there were anyone here we would have found them in our search."

Tis-ta-dae, agreeing, replied, "Well enough. However, to be safe, we will leave at the first light and soon be in Mexico on our way to the stronghold."

The two Apaches picked to scout El Paso did not know it but they had company on their journey. Shimitigua was following close behind. He negotiated the crevice down to the ground as soon as it was dark and followed them. Shimitigua moved along just behind and, at a large outcropping of rock about a mile east of the tanks, he turned to the left from the Butterfield Trail. He moved rapidly through the desert, his stride belaying his age.

He did not make as good a time as the Apaches since they were on a traveled road and he had to stick to wild terrain to avoid an encounter if there were other Apaches heading toward the Tanks. Shimitigua, upon reaching the Ysleta del Sur Pueblo, awoke the tribal leaders. A council was held between the War Captain, the Governor, the Cacique, and the old man. It was decided to immediately send a war party of Pueblo Indians to Hueco Tanks to pin the Apaches down while a messenger was sent to El Paso to tell the military that there were Apaches camped in their back yard.

The two Apache scouts reconnoitered El Paso then hurried back to the Tanks to report that there were no troops at El Paso other than a small security guard. The post had almost been emptied with the troops out on patrol pursuant to urgent commands being received from Colonel Hatch at Fort Cummings. They had been ordered by Hatch to block the Butterfield Trail west of El Paso.

The Apache scouts reached the Ysleta Y just ahead of the warriors coming from the Ysleta del Sur Pueblo. They were fortunate to detect them from the sound of the horses and pushed themselves hard to stay ahead of the Pueblo contingent. With only minutes to spare, they reached the Apache camp and sounded the warning, "We are about to be attacked!"

The Apaches put out their campfires, retreated into the great cave, and prepared to defend themselves.

The Pueblos attempted to surprise what they thought were sleeping Apaches but found only their gear and the hot coals of the fires. It was obvious that the Apaches were holed up in the cave. The Peublos positioned themselves to seal all possible escape. No shots were fired. No communication was had between one group of Indians and the other but each knew exactly what the other one was doing and why. They knew that the showdown would start with the break of dawn.

The Pueblo messenger told the officer in charge of the security guard at Fort Bliss that the Apaches were at Hueco Tanks. The officer quickly spread the word throughout the community. By morning there were thirty townspeople to lend support to the Pueblo Indians in their siege.

As soon as there was light to see by, the plan of attack was formulated. One group of Pueblos opened fire at the front of the cave and drew the attention of the trapped Apaches. As this was going on four Pueblo warriors worked their way to the right hand of the entrance to the cave through a crevice barely big enough to pass their bodies, hoping to reach the rear of the cave and surprise the Apaches. This strategy would have worked but for one of the defenders who was carrying out the orders of Tis-ta-dae to find an escape route. As a result, he was working his way through the same crevice only five feet above the Pueblos when he saw them. He immediately opened fire with a repeating carbine, killing one and wounding two others. Only one man was able to work his way out of the crevice unharmed.

This event sobered the besieging party into a deadly game of cat and mouse that was played out as the Pueblo Indians worked their way through other crevices hoping to find the passage into the main cave where they could position themselves to force the Apaches out into the waiting fire of the besiegers. The Pueblos, being very familiar with Hueco Tanks, knew that cracks crisscrossed the entire area. The trouble was there was no light in these passageways and you did not dare strike fire because you would be revealed to the enemy.

Old man Shimitigua had returned to Hueco Tanks the afternoon of the first day of the siege. After the Pueblo warrior was slain, Shimitigua laid out a plan for the next morning that he said would have a better chance of working. Shimitigua knew Hueco Tanks better than any other living man, having spent many spiritual retreats there. In the process, he had explored many of the fractures and knew of a route to the rear of the cave.

He was worn out from his ordeal on the trip to Ysleta and was not up to the effort required to navigate the passageways. He told a group of Tiguas of the route he thought they could take that would lead to surprise. In order to squeeze through the rock formations, four slender warriors were chosen. They had to remove their shirts and britches to make the effort. The Pueblo Indian delegated to lead the group was Demasio Colmenero, a young man of twenty-two with wisdom beyond his age.

The group started through a small seam pointed out by Shimitigua and gradually worked their way fifty feet into the mountain. At this point Shimitigua had instructed them to sharply turn left where they would lose all light. The infiltrating Pueblos easily reached the point with a large fissure to the left. They confirmed that Shimitigua's predictions were correct for the light was quickly lost. The passageway became steeper and the warriors had to break through a crust of debris of broken rock, twigs, sticks, and rat dung, constantly shifting and compacting.

The Pueblos inched forward on their bellies one in back of another keeping contact through touch and occasionally a low voice communication. Shimitigua had told them that after the steep incline, in a few feet they would find another fissure to the right and then a decline that would lead to a position immediately over the main chamber of the cave in which the Apaches were holed up.

Demasio paused and confirmed that all of his party was together and then signaled that they would begin their final descent. When Demasio started to the right, the other three were in close contact and the climb down began with the hope of their being in a position directly over the Apaches after forty feet of crawling.

The Apaches had discovered the same connecting passageway and had lifted three braves to the roof of the cavern on the backs of other Indians and were themselves exploring the passageway to see if it would lead to the outside. They had gone far enough up the incline to be totally out of the dim light that reached the portion of the cave where the Apaches had started their exploration.

In this black void the three Apaches and four Pueblos cautiously and slowly crawled toward each other climaxing in a head-on encounter. It was Demasio who first sensed that something was amiss. He was inches from physical contact with Chumascado who was point for the Apaches.

Demasio froze, reacting to a premonition of the presence of someone else. When he did, it took a second for those following him to realize that he was no longer moving forward. In that brief time, their stopping generated a faint noise from flesh and cloth scraping on rock. Alerted by the sound, Tis-ta-dae realized they were not alone in the passageway and he instinctively plunged forward with a knife in his right hand. The blow was delivered with great force, the blade passing completely through the hand of Demasio before breaking on the rock. Demasio let out a shout of surprise more than of pain.

Demasio's outburst led to a wild melee with the Apaches and Pueblos frantically trying to retreat and extricate themselves from what they perceived as a deadly ambush. Working their way head first through the narrow passageways had been a difficult job. Retreating in a panic backwards over the same course proved to be a near impossibility. The Apaches had less distance to travel to reach safety. They dropped out of the passageway down on to the floor of the cave one on top of the other. They swore the passageway was filled with Pueblo Indians heavily armed who would momentarily be in a position to attack the Apaches.

The Apaches watched both the mouth of the cave and the fissure in the roof, expecting the last attack to begin at any moment and knowing that they were heavily outnumbered. The attack never came from above. The Apaches didn't know it, but the Pueblos were hopelessly jammed in the second turn of the series of crevices they had negotiated. The last man in line had become confused and tried to go to his right instead of his left and was blocking the crevice at that point. As a result, the Pueblos were locked in a tangle of arms and legs angrily, in low voices, telling each other to clear the way so to stop obstructing the escape, all the while expecting the Apaches to fall upon them.

Demasio finally calmed everyone down and figured out what was happening after talking to Bernardo Holguin, now the lead Indian. He told him, "Go forward. You have made a wrong turn."

The minute Bernardo did this he realized his error and was

able to negotiate the rest of the trail to the daylight. The other Indians profited from his mistake and backed into the other crevice so they could turn around and complete their journey headfirst. In less than a minute they were all outside in the daylight excitedly telling their companions that the fissures and crevices of Hueco Tanks were filled to overflowing with Apaches bent and determined to kill any and all intruders.

"Shimitigua," Demasio said, "You have been wrong or else substantial Apaches have joined the first group while you were on your way to Ysleta."

The fellow besieger and onlookers could well believe the tale the Pueblos told as their bodies were bruised and bleeding from head to toe. In their mad scramble for safety they had repeatedly torn and cut themselves on the jagged rocks on the passageway they had been crawling in. Shimitigua applied first aid to Demasio's shattered hand.

Despite the Pueblo's miscalculation of Apache strength, the condition of Nana's band was becoming desperate as more and more besiegers congregated at Hueco Tanks. The Indian Pueblo at Ysleta was almost deserted as everyone, including the women and children, came out to watch the spectacle. Many of the townspeople from El Paso were also arriving anxious to see the end of the dreaded Apache raiders.

The Pueblos decided to try a novel strategy to drive the Apaches out into the open. They waited until dark, crawled up to the mouth of the cave, and left a pile of sticks, green brush and several bags of chili pods. They were jalapeno chilies, the hottest fruit of the valley gardens.

When the pile was complete a torch was applied, lighting up the night. The Indians fell back fifty yards where they ignited other bonfires before retreating to hiding places in the rocks. The strategy was that the acrid smoke would drive the Apaches out into the open where they could be picked off in the light of the bonfires.

A half hour later the besieged Apaches were ready to give up. The chili smoke was worse than tear gas and the Indians could not see. They were all beginning to retch and it was difficult to breathe. Tis-ta-dae was deliberating how to surrender without being massacred, when one of the braves who had been scouting for an escape route reported that he had found a passageway which led to the outside, but the outside opening was two-thirds up the face of a cliff. The Indian reported that the passageway was also free of smoke and chili poison.

Tis-ta-dae gathered his group together and they followed the explorer back to his discovery. Tis-ta-dae stretched his body outside the opening in the cliff face to see if he could find a handhold or anything to grasp in an escape attempt. The night was pitch black except for the stars which was blessing as far as their stealth was concerned but a curse on the ability to see.

They didn't dare light a torch because this would immediately alert the Pueblos and expose their escape attempt. Tis-ta-dae eased his way back into the passageway and reported his dilemma to Lozen. "I'm afraid that there is nothing to hold on to in order to reach the top of the cliff. If we knot our clothing and form a rope to drop down, we will be in the middle of our attackers."

"Surely" replied Lozen, "There must be a handhold somewhere within reach."

"Not that I could find," was Tis-ta-dae's response.

Lozen thought for a moment and then suggested, "Perhaps you can provide me with a platform using your body so that I can explore higher up the cliff than you were able to reach."

Tis-ta-dae thought the suggestion a wild gamble but at wits end to save his companions acceded. "Very well. But be cautious. There is no light other than the stars."

Tis-ta-dae inched out of the passageway on his stomach with his hands braced on the cliff wall while two companions held his legs, providing Lozen with as large a platform as he could.

Lozen crawled out on the top of Tis-ta-dae's back and was able to slowly stand erect. With her hands she explored the cliff face.

Lozen whispered to Tis-ta-dae, "There is a small tree here the size of my arm. It appears to be growing out of a crevice. I can barely reach it."

Tis-ta-dae answered, "Be careful. Come back down."

With them both back in the passageway Tis-ta-dae said, "Wonderful, I'll tear my tunic and make straps for you to use as a rope. Try to throw it over the tree and perhaps by some miracle there will be additional handholds further up."

Lozen assented and Tis-ta-dae deftly knotted a rope from strips of his shirt and again braced himself out of the passageway providing a platform for Lozen. She repeated her careful maneuver and stood up on the back of Tis-ta-dae and was able to toss the rope over the protruding trunk of Juniper. Lozen, using the rope, climbed up to the Juniper tree and standing on its trunk, was able to feel the slit in which the tree was growing which then widened sufficiently for handholds. Lozen whispered softly, "There is an opening wide enough for a hand to grab the rock, I am going to climb higher."

Lozen was able to find adequate purchase in the cliff and slowly inched her way up hand over hand. Gradually, the crevice spread and the cliff drifted from its vertical plane to a passable incline where Lozen was able to climb on her hands and knees to the top of the rock formation.

Satisfied the escape was possible, she negotiated her way back down and reported to Tis-ta-dae, "There is a way past the Juniper by using the opening in the rock the tree is growing in for handholds. It is about forty feet to where you can stand."

Tis-ta-dae did not hesitate and instructed the rest to negotiate Lozen's route one at a time.

The Apaches eagerly ascended, savoring the possibility of avoiding their tormentors. With Lozen leading the way, one by one they negotiated the escape route. Tis-ta-dae brought up the rear, removing the escape rope from the Juniper tree in case there was any temptation to follow.

The most difficult part of the escape was the effort to transport a wounded comrade up the cliff. The warrior had been hit in the gut by a bullet when the Pueblos first opened fire.

The experience taught the Apaches to retreat deeper into the cavern to avoid ricocheting lead. The wounded man was treated by Lozen. All she could do was make him comfortable and hope that internal injuries were minimal.

A harness was fashioned from straps made from tunics and a sling was fashioned to haul the injured warrior up the cliff face. He was next to the last man to leave the escape passageway and was steadied by Tis-ta-dae as his comrades gently pulled him up the face of the cliff.

Once on top it was obvious that the exertion had had dramatic consequences. The injured man had lapsed into unconsciousness and was undergoing spasms.

Tis-ta-dae directed his companions, "Move him into the clump of chamisa behind me and make him as comfortable as you can."

Lozen concurred, "Yes! That is all we can do. He will at least have a chance to survive. If we put him on a horse he would be dead in minutes."

A tunic that hadn't been torn up for harness was rolled and placed under the wounded man's head and the brush was arranged to give him shelter and hopefully prevent his discovery by the attackers.

Tis-ta-dae moved across the dome of rock and made for the side canyon where they had placed a bush barrier fence to hold their horses. Tis-ta-dae was amazed to find their animals still there and, in fact, all of the animals that the townspeople and the Pueblos had brought up to the tank were there with them. Most amazing of all, there was no guard; everyone was at the cave mouth waiting for the finale. Satisfied that the mounts really were unguarded, Tis-ta-dae instructed his companions, "Find your mounts and lead them out of here, the other animals will follow."

Tis-ta-dae led his pony out of the makeshift corral and the others followed eagerly picking their way down the gently inclining canyon floor of rocks and cactus as quietly as possible. Once free of the rock formation at Hueco Tanks they picked up their pace and headed towards the Rio Grande using the old Butterfield Trail and leaving a disappointed and horseless group behind.

Lozen was the last of the raiders to find her mount. Chubasco was in the rear of the rock enclosure when she located him. She ran her hands over his legs and body to make sure he was sound and ready to travel.

She grabbed his mane and vaulted on to his broad back then eased him down the rocky canyon floor by gentle tugs to the left and right on his mane. She pushed a dozen straggling mounts of the Pueblo Indians and townsmen ahead of her, leaving the makeshift corral vacant.

Once they cleared the Tanks, Lozen leaned forward and softly whispered into Chubasco's ear, "My wonderful friend, you don't know how happy I am to be riding your strong back. I thought I would never see you again. I believed we would die at the hands of the Pueblos."

Chubasco picked up his gait in response to a nudge from Lozen's heels and Lozen again whispered, "Faithful friend I have no need of a husband or children. How could any family be the equal of your trust and service to the Apache cause?"

A gentle tap of her heels launched Chubasco into a lope. In no time she had caught up with her escaping brothers.

When they reached the Ysleta Y they veered left for the Rio Grande where Tis-ta-dae confided to Lozen riding by his side, "I hope to never again set sight on that rock pile."

Lozen's response was, "Thank Ussen for our deliverance."

Apache Tears

CHAPTER FIFTEEN

Geronimo Surrenders

When Nana's band returned to the Netdahe stronghold they rested for many weeks, not wanting to put their heads in the noose that was being prepared for them by the angry Americans. Their inactivity was interrupted by a curious event. In the middle of the afternoon word spread through the Apache camp that two white eyes, a man and a woman, were coming up the zigzag trail, accompanied by an Apache. The news was met with disbelief. No white-eyes had ever penetrated this inner most recess of Apacheria.

A counsel was hastily called and Juh, Geronimo, Nana, Tis-ta-dae, and Lozen each commented on what should be done in this unusual emergency. Juh was for rolling boulders down upon them immediately as they came up the trail to end once and for all any intrusion into his domain. Cooler heads prevailed and it was decided to wait and see what it was they wanted.

Lozen guessed correctly that it had something to do with the young boy who had been brought as a prisoner a week earlier after a raid into New Mexico by Nacho, an uncontrollable Netdahe warrior who was trying to assert himself and obtain a position in the hierarchy of the Southern Apaches. The party was allowed to pass and, when they asked counsel with the Chiefs, were brought before Juh, Nana, Tis-ta-dae, and Geronimo, the dominant leader, wise and respected, who, while offered Chiefdom, had always turned it down, preferring to be a man of medicine. Lozen joined the counsel and looked at the woman sitting before them. She had red hair that glinted like burnished gold in the sun and green eyes that flashed fire when she stared at you. The man was a few years older but of commanding stature and great poise. They explained that they had come to seek the release of the woman's son and told how they had befriended the Apache and done all they could to prevent the cruelty of the whites towards the Apache people.

A young Indian girl broke from the Apaches gathering around the conference and ran to the young woman, shouting in Apache, "Lilly, Lilly, oh how wonderful to see you. How is my sister, Natasha? Tell me about her, please."

The Apaches instantly knew who this woman was. This was the lady who had befriended the two Apache girls, the sister and niece of Tis-ta-dae, the only survivors from a massacre by miners in the Gila Mountains.

After the counsel had received the request of the white-eyes, they entered into a long discussion with Juh opting to kill them both at once and Tis-ta-dae urging that they be spared. Finally Geronimo turned to Lozen and said, "Little sister, what is your wish with respect to this red-headed woman of the white-eyes?"

Lozen stood to emphasize her comments and said, "Goy ka la," using his Indian name, "To me, it is clear that this is a woman who has been good to the Apaches. We are hated by everyone only because we fight for what is ours. We have this chance to show everyone that we are just. And I say, let her have her son and let's give her freedom just as we want the same for ourselves."

With these remarks, Juh stood up, very resentful that a woman would be permitted to speak in a counsel of Apache leaders, and strode from the group toward the Netdahe encampment on the opposite edge of the clearing.

Shortly, everyone could hear the great drum sounding from the Netdahe camp. Geronimo cut the meeting short and standing, said, "It is well that you leave." To Nana he said, "Bring the boy at once and see that they are safely down the trail." Nana nodded assent.

Morning Mist and Tis-ta-dae stood at the head of the trail as they watched the two white-eyes go down with the boy they had come to rescue. Twice, when the beautiful woman turned back to wave, Morning Mist waved and called to her in Apache, "Say hello to my little sister. Give her my love and tell her I will join her when I can."

A day after this event Juh still feeling rebuked by the other Apache leaders and, with his Netdahe outnumbered and unable to assert his dominance, announced that he was going to Janos to enjoy a few nights. Three braves left with him in spite of the warnings of everyone not to trust the Mexicans as they believed that some day they would turn on him. He left to revel in a big drunk, a vice that this great Chief would soon carry to his grave.

Four days later the three warriors who had accompanied Juh to Janos appeared at the stronghold with the tragic news of Juh's death. They had stayed with Juh as he caroused for three days in the cantinas of Janos, making sure that no one took advantage of him. Juh had an amazing relationship with the townspeople. They were so afraid of retribution from his followers that they permitted him to come into town and frequent the cantinas. In exchange, he promised immunity to the town itself. This strange truce did not extend to patrols of soldiers stationed in town or the town's militia if they encountered Apaches in the field.

Juh's companions had finally persuaded him to start back for the stronghold. Juh agreed to return but insisted on riding all night. Near midnight, as they entered the rougher part of the Sierra Madre riding along a steep trail which dropped off into a fast rushing mountain stream, Juh fell from the saddle, striking his head on the rocks below the trail and winding up in the ice-cold stream with his face down. His companions rushed to him and, with some difficulty, supported his head above the water so that he could breathe. As soon as was possible, they dragged him onto the edge of the bank covering him with their blankets. After a short vigil, they noticed Juh's breathing becoming more and more labored and they feared the worst. They remained with their fallen leader, watching helplessly as his life ebbed away. They placed his body across his horse and brought him back to the stronghold where everyone was devastated by such sad news. Juh had been a great leader, a peer of the greatest, including Mangas Colorado, Cochise, Victorio, Nana, and his ancestor, Mahko.

The burial ceremony commenced immediately. The drums reverberated their mournful message across the canyon walls. Runners were sent out to bring in all of the hunting parties. The following day Juh was laid to rest halfway down from the mountain in a canyon wall in a deep crevice with rocks cascaded on top of him to close the fissure and forever protect his spirit.

After Juh had been buried the tribal elders met several times. A lively debate ensued as to what they should do. There were those that felt that they should hold out forever in the desolate mountains of the Sierra Madre and fight to the last person, preserving their heritage. There were others who were tired of being separated from their families and friends and realized that the tribe was dwindling more every day. While they killed ten white-eyes for every Apache lost the white-eyes kept coming and coming, and seemed to be without end.

Geronimo, now the dominant leader, vacillated back and forth. He had no love for the white-eyes; the Mexicans were his greatest enemy and they too were pressing closer every day. It was obvious that with the white-eyes now coming south of the border pursuing the Apaches ever closer, the day would soon come when they would, like rats, be cornered and exterminated.

During all of these counsels, Geronimo called upon Lozen to tell them whether they were safe or not as they moved from sanctuary to sanctuary. Lozen always gave them reassurances that there was no danger until one afternoon when the counsel met. She made her incantations and entered a trance and then announced that they were in grave peril, both from the Mexicans and the Americans who were coming ever nearer.

Geronimo sent Lozen and another woman, Tah-das-te, to Fronteras to bargain with the Mexicans for peace terms. When they returned, they had information that the Mexicans were willing to talk. However, two Chihenne warriors, Kaytinah and Martin, were close on their trail carrying a message from Lieutenant Gatewood to come in for a peace parley.

Shortly after Lozen's arrival at the stronghold with her message from the comandante at Fronteras, lookouts reported the two Apaches coming up the trail behind her. They were recognized immediately as former allies who had joined the ranks of the detested scouts working for the white-eyes. A lively discussion ensued as to whether or not they should be killed or permitted to enter the camp.

It was obvious to Lozen that Geronimo was fast losing heart and he asked her, "Little sister, what should we do?"

She replied, "I think there is nothing else we can do. Our day is at an end. At least let's be with our family and friends."

Geronimo nodded his head in assent and said, "Yes, that is how I feel too."

He ordered that the scouts were to be permitted to pass. They approached and told him that Lt. Gatewood was waiting down below to discuss a surrender with him.

Geronimo gave orders to break the camp and everyone quickly stored their gear, loaded the pack animals, and gathered in their mounts and spares. When Geronimo felt the time was right, he, Nana, and Tis-ta-dae went down the zigzag trail to meet Lt. Gatewood below. A lively discussion ensued and Geronimo, who trusted the Lieutenant, asked him what he would have him do.

The reply was, "There is no choice but to surrender. You will be treated well. And General Miles, who is an honest man, will not harm you."

With this assurance Geronimo gave his assent and the remnants of the Southern Apaches gathered at the bottom of the zigzag trail. When they were all there Geronimo inquired after several of his best braves and was told they had stayed behind with their families and were determined to last it out.

He shrugged his shoulders and said, "So be it."

He accompanied Lt. Gatewood twelve miles to a camp where there was a large American Cavalry detachment which had been bent on taking Geronimo in the stronghold. Here conferences were held and Geronimo proceeded with the military escort to a meeting with General Miles. Lozen followed behind, sad in her heart that she was to witness the end of the Apaches. She frequently glanced back into the Blue Mountains of Old Mexico, realizing that she would never again see a place where Apaches were wild and free. Nana rode by her side, occasionally wiping a tear from his eyes. The old warrior was so crippled by arthritis that he could only ride with great difficulty. But had he been given a choice, he would not have surrendered. He did not have the compulsion of Geronimo to be with his wives and children.

Tis-ta-dae rode in back of Nana and Lozen and, like them, frequently looked back, wishing that he had elected to stay behind with the ones that wanted to go on with the fight but, bound by loyalty to Nana, his mentor, he must accompany him into whatever hell might await the Apaches.

When they reached the campsite of General Mills, Geronimo called a halt and told Lt. Gatewood that he wished to speak to his people before he actually surrendered. The first instructions he gave were to Lozen.

"My little sister, go back and mingle with the women. I do not want the white-eyes to know who you are because it may be that the warriors will be killed. If that is the case, you should survive and bear witness to treachery."

Lozen protested saying, "No. No. I am with you. I am prepared to die. I want to die if that is the fate of my brothers."

"No," Geronimo insisted, "I order you to join the women now and keep your voice still. You should not be known to the white-eyes as the sister of Victorio. Your name should never be spoken by other Apaches. Go now. I will hear no more."

Lozen realized it was futile so she joined the women and children as Geronimo negotiated the final surrender of the Apache Nation, the last gasp of Indian sovereignty.

Geronimo met with General Miles in Skeleton Canyon. The Apaches camped a hundred yards from where General Miles was already established with the cavalry detachment. The Indians were on the higher ground and scattered out so that they could beat a hasty retreat if it proved that the peace conference was a hoax. They arrived in the middle of the afternoon. Geronimo sent some of the warriors in to visit with the Apache scouts and Army officers while he stayed in camp and waited for reports on the tone of the potential conclave. In the meantime, four of the Apache scouts visited the camp of the holdouts. Geronimo and Nana were very uneasy about the traitors visiting with the mixed band of Indians who were considering a surrender to General Miles. There were ties of kinship and friendship and a common desire to end the exasperating life on the run that the Apaches had endured ever since the outbreak in 1876. Nonetheless, apprehension was high. No one trusted the white-eyes and no one trusted the Apaches who had taken up with them.

That evening as darkness settled over the Indian camp Geronimo asked Lozen to come to his camp where she found Geronimo and Nana contemplating their choices.

As Lozen walked up and appeared in the circle of the fire Geronimo stood up and said, "Welcome, sister. Come sit in counsel with Nana and me. We need your sage advice."

Nana had also arisen as Lozen came into view, a mark of the extreme deference in which Lozen was held by all Apaches, and added his greeting, "Yes, little sister and mother of Apaches, come join us. We need your advice on how we are to proceed."

Nana sat down and poked a stick into the fire, stirring the coals into bright embers.

Lozen sat between the two and gazing into the fire, said, "I wish that there were words of advice I could give you that would be of help to our people. But I fear that all is lost and that we are doomed to follow a lonely trail that winds down the canyon and is lost in the memories of what we were."

Geronimo looked at her sharply and said, "You are saying my words and, because of that, I fear that we are indeed lost. Nana, do you share this fear that we are on the last of our journeys?"

Nana stirred the fire again and looked at Lozen and then Geronimo and then leaned forward on one knee and raised both arms to the sky saying, "Ussen, we have followed you always and always will, but it seems that we and you are finally at the end of our trail. Lozen who is with us has many of your powers. She has been blessed by you, more so than all of us combined. Speak to us through her and let us know what we must do."

Lozen looked at Nana and slowly wiped a tear that was welling down her cheek. She pursed her lips and grimly clinched her teeth as she looked skyward. Instead of raising her arms she crossed them over her chest and said, "Oh, Ussen, please tell us we are wrong. That there is another way."

She continued her gaze skyward for a minute then cast her eyes down and, settling back on the log, turned to Geronimo and said, "You are the head of my family and I have no way of saying you are wrong. I wish with all my heart that there was something we could do to keep our people alive. But with the white-eyes like grains of sand throughout the Blue Mountains and our homeland, I know of nothing we can do except submit to what must be and I join in your counsel that we surrender to General Miles."

Geronimo had never been seen to cry but with this declaration by Lozen, he wiped his eyes and nodded to her while he reached over with his right hand and clasped her left saying, "Yes, little sister, we are all locked in the same cave. There is no other way but let me warn you that you are not to be with us when we meet with the General. Nana and I will meet with the other braves but I want none of the white-eyes to know who or what you are. They do not know you and I do not want them to know that there is a woman among us who can see the future. Let them think you are part of the baggage we carry. Otherwise, surely your life will be in danger."

Nana rose and grasped Lozen by the hand and, pulling her up, took hold of her other hand and holding her firmly said, "Yes, my daughter, especially you I wish to save. Do not give a single sign of recognition as we do tomorrow what must be done. Although we will surrender, Ussen will work his ways through you. Let not the white-eyes know who you are."

The next morning Geronimo, Nana, and the other warriors walked down the canyon and sat with General Miles and arranged the surrender which was little more than acquiescence. The only commitment that they had received from Lt. Gatewood was that they would not be tried or hanged but would join their families and have their fates decided by the great white father in Washington. They outnumbered the soldiers two to one and would gladly have put them all to death but to what avail?

Still, Geronimo tried to bargain with Miles and seek a promise of reservation life in New Mexico, even the dreaded San Carlos Reservation if that was all that was left in the way of an option but Miles stood fast and said "No. The terms are clear. Your lives will be spared and you will join your families and be subject to the will of the president but nothing else can be promised you."

Miles lacked the empathy that General Crook had held towards Indians and the Indians realized at once that this was a different man that they were speaking with but that did not change the awesome reality that they had played the game to the end and they were left with no recourse. Geronimo did insist that he and some members of the band would not accompany the general back to the reservation at this time but would join them promptly. Miles was furious that the surrender was not complete but finally reluctantly agreed.

When the ceremonies were over, Geronimo and Nana returned to the Apache camp and told everyone there to accompany General Miles to the reservation while he and Nana and five warriors picked by him would return to the stronghold and seek out the other families whom they had not been able to notify of the meeting and surrender. Geronimo immediately broke camp and with his party headed back towards the Blue Mountains of the Sierra Madre. For the next sixty days they fanned out and found all of the Apaches that were in seclusion in Mexico. Of these some thirty individuals, twelve members of three families decided to stay behind and fend for themselves in the home range of the Netdahe. In addition, Chief Naiche and seven others, including the son of Juh, said that they would surrender on their own. Geronimo realized that there was some resentment of him as a leader because he had never been formally proclaimed a Chief, so he agreed to this course of action.

Geronimo and Nana, with heavy hearts, rode down the zigzag trail for the last time and cut North across the Sonoran Desert towards the dreaded San Carlos Reservation. They were accompanied by twenty-five other Apaches, including Warm Springs, Chiricahua, and Mescalero. Behind them in the Sierra Madre, they left a few lonely Apaches to carry the torch and remain a symbol of freedom but with the promise and commitment to Geronimo that they would cease and halt all depredations and raids in order to ensure the safety of those who had surrendered. This was a promise that they would keep.

The first group of surrendering Apaches, including Lozen, were taken under cavalry escort to the San Carlos agency on the San Carlos River in Arizona. The agency was a hot desert environment of cactus and cat's claw wholly foreign to the Warm Springs mountain environment.

Once they arrived the warriors were separated and thrown into the stockade as prisoners of war. The Warm Springs scouts who had led the military on its final missions to subdue the Apaches were also disarmed and thrown in the stockade to be transferred to a prison in Florida.

Lozen escaped the ignominy of imprisonment at San Carlos and the authorities, not knowing her status, let her associate with the women and children still enjoying the freedom of movement about the agency.

When they reached San Carlos the Apache mounts were confiscated and placed in the cavalry remuda. Lozen was able to visit her friend Chubasco and scoured the San Carlos River bottoms for tufts of green grass and herbs to take to her friend who was otherwise restricted to moldy hay and contaminated grain.

When Geronimo, true to his vow, finally surrendered, word spread that the captives would be taken by wagon to Holbrook, Arizona and placed on a train bound for Florida. When Lozen received this information she was shattered. The thought of imprisonment in a distant land was devastating. Most galling was that, inevitably, she would be forced to part with her friend Chubasco. With her entire family gone Chubasco was all that she had near and dear.

Soon after she heard the news, Lozen slipped down to the river and gathered greens as a treat for Chubasco. Chubasco saw her coming up the riverbank and let out a soft bray as he hurried to the pole fence to visit with his mentor. Hearing Chubasco, Lozen ran as fast as she could to be with her friend. She vaulted the fence and, before sharing her treats, reached her arms around his neck and hugged him with all of her might and, almost shouting said, "I have terrible news. Word is spreading through the agency that tomorrow we leave for a place called Florida."

The mule, sensing her urgency, stepped forward, as he wanted to be as close to her as he could, forcing her to step back. Lozen continued her outburst, "My beloved friend, I will die without you. You have safely seen me through every ordeal."

Now, in sobbing tears, Lozen exhorted her friend, "Never forget me; there is nothing in life, including life itself, that I treasure as I treasure and love you."

At that moment the sergeant in charge of the stables came from behind the barn and, seeing Lozen with Chubasco, exclaimed, "Hey there, I've told you and told you to stay away from that mule."

The sergeant advanced with authority towards the pair causing Lozen to step back. The sergeant barked gruffly, "Come on now, get out of here."

Lozen did not understand the sergeant's words but his tone of voice and his flailing arms made it clear that she was being forced to leave her faithful companion. She turned and crossed the corral and stood in total disarray looking at Chubasco who was pushing against the poles trying to nuzzle her. The sergeant raised his quip and struck Chubasco a sharp blow on the rump causing him to turn and bolt back into the swarming remuda which was disturbed by the sergeant's gruff voice. As Lozen saw Chubasco disappear into a cloud of dust raised by the animals' hooves, she cupped her hands and shouted, "Farewell good friend," After a pause, "I love you!"

Lozen turned and ran back to the agency, a distraught and shaken woman who knew that a vibrant episode of her life was over.

CHAPTER SIXTEEN

Prisoners of War

The surviving Southern Apaches were loaded onto wagons and taken on a two-day trip to Holbrook, Arizona, where they were entrained for Florida. There were no escapes from this train. This was the last of the Apache scourge on its way to oblivion and the white-eyes made sure that there was no opportunity for diversion. On reaching Florida, there was great joy and excitement as they joined their families and friends and also anguish and lamentation as all of the Apaches realized that they were no longer a free and independent people.

Lozen, like everyone else that had just made the trip to Florida, was excited to see her friends and relations. It was a wonderful reunion. But the thrill was gone the next morning when Lozen awoke and realized that there was a heavy presence in the air. She had never experienced humidity and, like the other Apaches, had great difficulty breathing freely with all the moisture being taken into her lungs. Not only the air was strange but also the scenery was totally alien. What would have been dear to the eyes and hearts of a Seminole was cruel and suspect to an Apache. The palm trees, the vines, the low lying oaks, the moss falling in shreds towards the ground, gave the Apaches the impression of having been doomed by Ussen to a life in hell.

Some of the Apaches had been there for six months, others for lesser periods but Lozen quickly found out that a common complaint was that most of them were ill. This sickness spared no one, the old, young, and the babies were all ill. Some were racked with fever and then chills followed by total disability. Others were tormented with horrible coughs and expulsions of sputum laced with blood as they tried to clear their lungs.

Lozen took charge of the ill and organized teams to care for them. She insisted that everyone who was well take on a role. This bothered many of the men who had never been subjected to orders from a woman but not those who had served with Lozen and knew her abilities. Geronimo and fierce old Nana saw to it that everyone responded to the will of Lozen and, within a week of her arrival, there was a hospital functioning on the grounds of the old fort.

Within two or three days after the hospital was organized, the Army medical doctor showed up and was amazed to see that the Apaches had organized themselves to assist the ill. He made repeated inquiry as to who had engineered such a resourceful effort but never was told that it was Lozen who had put her print upon the organization at Fort Marion. Geronimo and the Chiefs had spread the word that Lozen was not to be identified; that the white-eyes were not to know the role she had played in the conflict in the Southwest.

Two of Lozen's nieces were ill with tuberculosis and were in her makeshift hospital, coughing away their young lives. Lozen was desperate to be of assistance to them and the other Apaches that were ill but nothing she did caused them to respond. A month after arriving at Fort Marion, her heart was heavy as she buried the first niece and then, a week later, the second. The other Apaches were suffering and dying in the same fashion. The effort of the white-eyes to conquer the Apaches in the deserts and the mountains of the Southwest was totally ineffectual but this new weapon was decimating the Indians. It mattered not what you did to help the patient either lived or died depending upon their constitution and raw chance. None of the Indian remedies were available in this strange new land and care and love and attention were the only medicine that could be administered.

The Chiefs were furious with the American officers who came to visit their prison, insisting that they had been betrayed and that the Apaches were being killed in a far more cruel fashion than the hangman's noose. Finally there was some hope when it was announced that they were moving to a place in a land called Alabama. It was a horrible disappointment when they arrived at Mt. Vernon Barracks and found conditions to be identical to those they had left behind in Florida.

As soon as they arrived at this new lodging Lozen took charge and had one of the buildings functioning as a hospital. The Army doctor was very grateful for Lozen's assistance and cooperated with her fully, teaching her how to administer the few medications that were available. The sergeant in charge of the camp could see that this woman exercised unusual influence over the other Apaches and repeatedly asked questions of the scouts as to why she was so prominent. To a man, the Indians expressed total ignorance, knowing that their lives would not be worth a plugged nickel if Geronimo and Nana ever even suspected that they had betrayed Lozen as a leader of the Warm Springs Apaches.

Lozen plunged into her work, aware that this was part of her task in life. Relying on Ussen she gave of herself totally and completely.

Lozen and the Army doctor did everything they could to expand their little hospital to take care of all the sick Indians. If they had been able to accommodate everyone who was suffering from tuberculosis or yellow fever, the hospital would have been flooded and three-fourths of the tribe would have been patients. Handling the children sent back from Carlyle Indian school was a major task. When a child was sent back to its parents, it was for one reason only and that was because it was going to die. It didn't take the Apaches long to figure out that, when their children came back, the white men were just granting one final indulgence and that was death among the family.

It wrenched Lozen's heart to see the youngsters come back spitting blood and gradually growing weak with the racking cough that the tuberculosis left in its wake. The afflicted wasted away to shadows, mere skeletons clothed with skin. Seized with agonizing pain, they died the worst of deaths.

The yellow fever victims were just as pathetic and, while the two diseases were totally dissimilar, the victims in the end were reduced to the same abject lethargy. The doctor could do nothing. Lozen could do nothing except to make their patients comfortable and keep them clean. No one knew the source of these dread scourges. Every day they were all repeatedly bitten by the mosquito carriers of the yellow fever while they constantly inhaled the airborne bacilli of tuberculosis.

From the afflicted Indians at Mt. Vernon Barracks, there would be survivors, Apaches who, by chance, had some resistance to these horrible scourges of the Europeans. Those few who did not contract either malady were the forerunners of a genetic disposition to reject the infections. Lozen herself had been infected for two years before the symptoms began to debilitate her. She not only had the deadly tuberculin bacterium but yellow fever infection as well. Her magnificent constitution had spared her the suffering and torment incidental to the onslaught of both much longer than normal.

The Army doctor had repeatedly told her to wear a gauze mask and had instructed her on the things she should do to prevent the tuberculosis infection to herself. Lozen ignored all of his cautions and pressed on with her administering to the ill with complete disregard for her own wellbeing. Her stamina and strength were outstanding and for four years she was doctor, nurse, and father confessor to the one-half of the tribe that was continually ill. And then, during the fifth year, it happened. One morning Lozen woke up and began to cough. At first gently, and then with an explosion that brought sputum and blood and she knew that she had become terminally ill. Her sickness accelerated and within six weeks she was lying in her bed at death's door.

When it became evident to Dr. Hamilton that Lozen herself was critically ill he did all he could to slow her down and make her rest but it was to no avail. She was determined to fight for her people. And every night after a hard day of tending to the hopelessly dying, she would at last lie down wrapped in her blanket and wonder what it was that she was trying to do and why. Here were her people totally cast upon a refuse pile. Not only were their culture and traditions denied but also they were placed in an environment which was hostile to their own. She just couldn't understand what it was that was happening. *Would not it have been better to have been lined up, man, woman, and child, in New Mexico and shot by the firing squad? Why did Ussen permit this disaster? Are we being punished? What has gone wrong?*

Surely that form of death was far more gentle than the abominable torture they faced daily. Even the well were despondent, depressed, and unable to function. At last, the white European society had overcome the Native American culture. There was nothing left now but death, disease, and despair.

Dr. Hamilton had grown fond of Lozen. She was like the nurses he had known, totally devoted to the welfare of others. Sacrificing themselves at every step. Finally, to preserve that one flickering flame of hope, he ordered Lozen to bed herself and forbade her to tend to any other.

Lozen had always obeyed. First her mother and father and then her brother and then Nana and Juh and Geronimo. All had fallen. And she knew in her heart that, while Dr. Hamilton was not an Apache, he was a good man and trying to help them and one who knew more than anyone else what was wrong.

The doctor had arranged for a permanent assignment at Mt. Vernon Barracks knowing that there was no one else to carry on the Herculean chores assumed by Lozen. Once Lozen was too ill to move about and help anyone else, she was forced onto an army cot wrapped in a blanket, where the doctor and his orderlies wiped her forehead and tried to keep her cool. She could only talk to the doctor through Nana and then it required another interpreter who spoke Spanish, but she still could communicate with her eyes and the movement of her lips and her hands. The doctor could communicate back by nodding affirmatively or negatively and touching her with great affection and moving his eyes and lips.

As Lozen's light lowered, her vital functions began to fade but the activity of her mind accelerated. Memories of her youth came flooding back. Visions of her family together in the remote, wild, free land of New Mexico inundated her mind and recollections flooded in. There was an Apache tradition that before you died you would see everything that had happened to you. That Ussen would review your life and let you know his judgment.

Lozen, who had never worried about what might happen to her, realized that she was on the final journey. As Lozen sank lower and lower her mind gravitated back to the start of the downfall of the Warm Springs. She remembered the warriors coming back from Camp Sherman with the captured horses and then the following day when Tis-ta-dae came in horribly wounded, his jaw shattered and his right leg almost useless. At that time Tis-ta-dae was a mere youth of fifteen while Lozen, herself, was in her mid twenties. She had been asked by Nana to help to administer to the young brave since Tis-ta-dae's mother was stricken by the bite of a rattlesnake. As her feverish mind roamed over the memories of the past, she recalled the shock she felt when Nana removed Tis-ta-dae's loincloth and exposed his body.

She had never before seen a man's body. Nana, himself, was so busy directing the activities of Lozen that he did not stop and realize that he was exposing a brave to the gaze of an Indian maiden. Even if he had realized it, he would have gone on because he knew what had to be done and so did Lozen, and somehow they worked together as a team, changing the dressings, and finally, miraculously, setting the jaw. Lozen wasn't sure of all the braces and splints that Nana employed but she could see that he was obviously trying to stabilize the broken bones so that they could heal.

In her hallucination, Lozen recalled the ordeal she herself had gone through after the wounds of Tis-ta-dae had been dressed by

Nana. All during the night following the doctoring, Tis-ta-dae had fought to rise up and tear away the splints and bindings. Lozen, alone, kept him down finally smothering his body with her own to be able to control the great strength the young boy possessed. When, in desperation, she lay on top of him trying to control his spastic reaction she realized that she enjoyed the contact. Though a functioning woman for many years, Lozen had resisted every overture from a male and had remained chaste. And yet here she was fantasizing sexually as she felt the warmth of Tis-ta-dae's body beneath hers. She could have raised up and somehow contended with his violent spasms but she instinctively knew it was far better if she kept him subdued, even though it evoked in her these powerful feelings of pleasure. She had seen his genitals when Nana had repacked the wound on his thigh, but she had kept them covered with buckskin ever since. And, while she was tempted to, in the privacy of administering to him, look again on his manhood, she held back. She knew that she would receive satisfaction in such a move but she also knew that she had a deeper devotion and that was to return him to the tribe. He was marked for greatness.

In her feverish delusions, Lozen slipped into a different zone of time and remembered when she had playfully tackled Tis-ta-dae in the Blue Mountains of Mexico. Their body contact had jolted her into remembering she was a woman. Two days later, she and Tis-ta-dae had met by accident late in the afternoon. As she was coming back from delivering a message to an Apache group camped on the opposite edge of the Copper Canyon abyss, she had met him returning from a hunt carrying a big buck on his shoulders. When they met it was too late to get back to camp so they had decided to share a bivouac together halfway up the zigzag trail to the stronghold. That night by a campfire they chatted and Lozen told Tis-ta-dae that she had been the one who had carried out the instructions of Nana to heal his grievous wounds. He had not known this.

He had, however, always instinctively been drawn to Lozen who, to him, was the ultimate woman. He had felt a male desire to be aggressive when Lozen had wrestled him to the ground two days earlier but not as they camped and visited. He looked at her in the firelight and realized that she had administered to him when he was on the verge of death. A new feeling overcame him. He was well aware that he, as a man of few moons, could not be involved romantically with a woman of many more years. And then for the first time in Tis-ta-dae's life he wanted to rebel. Why should he care how the Apaches felt? His life was his own and he had carnal desire to take this woman for his own. Little did he know that her feeling towards him to do the same was twice as strong. They both had resisted the temptation and played out the role that their culture demanded.

Word spread throughout the Warm Springs and Chiracahuas at Mt. Vernon Barracks that Lozen was dying. While Lozen had never been elected a Chief, she had risen in the esteem of her fellow Apaches to a level equal to that of any man. No one, man or woman, had ever sacrificed so totally, completely for the welfare of the Apache people. She was viewed as filling an all-encompassing role, both as a warrior and as a mother-father figure and, in addition, chosen by Ussen to share his powers.

Nana, Geronimo, and Tis-ta-dae took turns staying with Lozen night and day. Nana himself was skin and bones and stricken so with arthritis that he could hardly move without the help of others but he was determined to be with this amazing woman who had been his lifelong confidant and friend. In his last coherent conversation with Lozen she confessed, "My beloved protector, when I see all this misery and death, my faith in Ussen is shaken."

Nana cupped his hands under Lozen's chin and raised her face until their eyes were riveted. "Doubt not little sister," he spoke gently, "Apache Spirit includes faith in Ussen. He has his reasons for everything. We thrived in our homeland before the intruder came and we will control our own destiny again when they are gone."

Tis-ta-dae was one of the few Apaches that had not contracted any of the horrible illnesses that abounded in the swamps of Florida and Alabama and he was shocked to see Lozen so frail and dissipated. When she coughed, flecks of blood would fill the air.

On the second day of the vigil, Tis-ta-dae asked Lozen if she would like to go out in the sun, which was making a rare appearance over the Indian prison. She smiled briefly and nodded her assent and Tis-ta-dae picked her up in his strong arms and carried her out to a chair that had been fashioned from cane and vines. Tis-ta-dae placed her tenderly in the chair and sat down beside her, watching her soak up the warm, invigorating rays. The beneficial effect was immediate and an hour later when Lozen indicated that she needed to return to the shade, she was in much better spirits and could move her arms. For a few hours, hope sprang in the hearts of the three men and other members of the tribe who were now beginning to gather, that perhaps Lozen's life would be spared. While the others hoped that there had indeed been a change, Nana kept his own counsel for he, along with Geronimo, knew well that this was but a momentary improvement and that before the night was over, Lozen would end her journey through life and be free from all pain and suffering.

Tis-ta-dae did not realize that the end was so near and hoped with all his heart and conviction that this strange and powerful woman who had influenced his life so deeply would improve. He remembered the times that she had raced against him and the occasions when she had won. He could remember in particular a brief moment when they forgot the Apache customs and wrestled in the Blue Mountains of Old Mexico. Tis-ta-dae had attractions for this older woman that made him ashamed and uneasy. He could never understand what they were. She was his mother and then again she wasn't. She was his friend. But that did not include all of his feelings; comrade on the trail, partner in danger, and yet something more which Tis-ta-dae could not make sense out of. He had often thought that if she were in any way approachable, he would ask Nana for her hand. But the collective opinion of the Warm Springs and the other bands was that Ussen had sent Lozen on a course that set her apart from all other Apaches and made her unique, and that marriage did not fit into this plan. Tis-ta-dae did not know and would never believe Lozen would welcome his request for her hand

and that in this respect he was unique as she had never considered any other possible suitor.

As Lozen weakened, the doctor personally sat by her bed as she began the work of dying. At his side was Nana from whom Lozen had learned the secrets of medicine. The two watched Lozen's emaciated body convulse.

The next morning when the doctor came in to look upon his patient he found Nana by her side. Nana turned to the doctor when he came in and smiled. In Apache, he said, "Fear not. She is well now."

The Army doctor did not know what he had said but sensed that a crisis was at hand. He looked at Lozen and saw that she was asleep and very much at peace. Not a smile, but at least a calmness on her face.

Nana stood up and looked at Dr. Hamilton and said again in Apache, "Please leave us alone now. We must do Indian medicine to help our sister who is going to join Ussen."

The doctor was perplexed. He had no idea what Nana had said but knew that the end was near and that his job was over. He leaned over Lozen and put his hand upon her feverish brow. He then raised his right hand to his lips and kissed his fingers and placed them upon the lips of Lozen. His touch awakened her and she looked up at her friend and smiled. She raised her left hand in the air, groping for the doctor's which he clasped in both his hands. She then pressed with all the strength she had left, staring at him intently. The communication was electric and Hamilton knew that she was truly his friend.

He stood, turned, and walked out of the building and, standing in the sun, looked skyward and said, "Almighty God, I have come to know that you are one and the same for all of us. Take this good woman and give her peace and comfort. She has spent her life in the service of others."

As Lozen lay in her bed, for the last time her feverish mind wandered back through her life recalling with joy and sadness all the things she had seen and done and finally riveted on that moment when she was alone on the sacred mountain undergoing the ordeal of revelation into womanhood.

That day had shaped every remaining moment of her life, driving her to forsake all the normal pleasures. Now, with her body racked with pain, her lips twisted, cracking, trying to smile and give comfort to those who watched her death agony, she begged Ussen in silent prayer, *Reveal your purpose in giving me such power and give me a sign that I have fulfilled your mandate.* Hallucinating, her mind filled again with that wondrous vision of her dividing and dividing again, ever expanding to fill all space, only now each division intensified and Lozen, in revelation, understood that the dividing figures were not singularly herself but were representative of all Apaches who had gone before and would come after. Lozen's own insight then divined the full meaning of the vision: *All Apaches are joined in psychic unity.* It was clear to Lozen that the power had been given not to her but through her to the Apache people and that she was but the means by which Ussen gave his protection to all.

Peace settled upon Lozen, satisfied that she had fulfilled her destiny. She had never married or enjoyed life's normal pursuits and had instead become the instrument by which the gift of Ussen to the Apache people had been delivered. Lozen was satisfied. A life of service and devotion to the Apaches was well worth whatever she had been denied. At peace, Lozen closed her eyes and gave her powers back to Ussen.

As dawn broke, Nana, burdened with age and disease, leaned over the still body with bitter Apache tears streaming down his face. He spoke softly,

> **You are truly Nantan, a great Chief of the Apaches. We have lost our struggle to remain free yet our victory is great. The white-eyes take our land and our lives but they have not dimmed our Apache spirit. Go now, little sister, join the band of the dead and tend the last altar fire.**

Apache Tears

POSTSCRIPT

Nana and his raiders fought a battle with Lieutenant Guilfoille's detachment of cavalry in the vicinity of Mockingbird Gap which lies between the San Andreas and the Oscura Mountains within the White Sand Missile Range on the 25th day of July 1881. A mere 64 years later, 8 miles to the north at Trinity Site, the world's first atomic explosion took place on July 16, 1945.

Across the craggy peaks and desolate valleys of the Southwest, a proud people once held sway. They were the Apaches, the last Indians to reach the mountain and desert basin terrain of Texas, New Mexico, and Arizona. While the archaeological records are meager, it is generally believed that they shortly preceded the Spanish entradas that started with Coronado in 1540. Apache origins were in the west coast of Canada and Alaska where their athapaskan speaking kinsmen, the Haida and Clinket, still reside. Their masterful adaptation from a maritime climate to the harsh desert mountain environment mirrors their fashioning and mastery of the art of guerrilla warfare.

General Douglas MacArthur in his autobiography remembers being a youngster at Ft. Selden in the heart of Apacheria while his father was post commander. He credits the Apaches as being the finest light cavalry to ever take the field. Small wonder he would express such zeal when the combined armies of Mexico and the United States were held at bay by Southern Apaches during the last gasp of Indian sovereignty between 1876 and 1886. A mere handful of warriors repeatedly outfought and out-generaled the best that both countries could throw against them.

The Apaches were organized in bands which associated in larger allied groups. One of these was the Southern Apaches, masters of Southwestern New Mexico, Southeastern Arizona and large areas of northern Mexican states Chihuahua and Sonora. The Southern Apaches consisted of four closely related bands, two large and two small. The large bands were the Warm Springs and the Chiricahua. The Warm Springs called themselves the Chihenne for their red paint and they roamed the San Mateos, San Andreas, Black Range, the Eastern Mogollon Rim, the Floridas of New Mexico and the eastern Sierra Madre of Old Mexico. They summered in the mountain wilderness of their northern range and wintered in the lower valleys and foothills. Their principal rancheria was Warm Springs, 17 miles north of present day Winston, New Mexico. The Warm Springs were also historically known as the Copper Mine and Mimbres Apache. Their best-known chiefs were Mangas Colorado, Victorio, and Nana.

The Chiricahua ranged through the Chiricahua and Dragoon Mountains of southwestern New Mexico and southeastern Arizona across the desert floor to the southern escarpment of the Mogollon Mountains. They were called, by themselves and other Apaches, the Chokonen, the white paint people, after their custom of wearing white paint when at war. Their best-known chief was the legendary Cochise.

The two smaller bands were the Bedonkohe and Netdahe. The Bedonkohe ranged west of the Warm Springs in the eastern and middle fork drainage of the Gila River and into the San Francisco River drainage and the eastern flank of the Blue Mountains of Arizona. The Bedonkohe were the Bronze Paint people and Geronimo was their best-known leader.

The Netdahe held dominion in the Blue Mountains (Sierra Madre) of Old Mexico. They were the wildest and fiercest of the Southern Apaches and it was from their stronghold at the top of a zigzag trail that Geronimo directed the final convulsions of Apache resistance. Jason Betzeniz, who was forced by Geronimo to join the renegades and fight as an apprentice warrior in the final Apache campaign, tells us that the Netdahe were composed of members of many Apache bands and Navajos along with Mexicans who had been captured as children and raised in the Apache tradition. The best-known leader of the Netdahe was Juh, a masterful tactician who was married to Ishtee, the sister of Geronimo.

Many anthropologists today favor calling all of the Southern Apache bands Chiricahua, but this is not how the Indians refer to themselves.

To the west of the Southern Apache, the San Carlos and White Mountain Apaches held sway and were referred to in the early military accounts as the Western Apache and included the Tonto Apache and the Mojave Apache, a mixed group.

East of the Rio Grande and centered in the Tularosa basin and Sacramento Mountains were the Mescaleros with life styles similar to the Southern Apaches and their frequent allies. The Mescaleros, during the early Spanish colonial period, controlled the Guadalupe, Davis, and the Chisos Mountains and Basin of the Big Bend. Early Spaniards described their mescal pit fires on the southern slopes of the Guadalupes as stars in the sky, so numerous were their gathering camps.

The Mescaleros and the Lipan Apaches to their east are often referred to as the Eastern Apaches, but this is not an accurate grouping as the Lipan were adapted to a plains lifestyle. Lipan remnants are found on the Mescalero Reservation (repatriated from Mexico) and among the Tonkawa tribe of Oklahoma.

To the north of the Southern Apaches were the Jicarilla Apaches, a mountain dwelling band who largely escaped conflict with the Mexicans and experienced far less turmoil from the invading Americans than did other Apache groups. To the west of the Jicarilla in northwest New Mexico and in northern Arizona lived the Navajo, today the largest tribe in America. They are also Athapascan speakers and little differentiated from the other Apache groups.

The Southern Apaches and, in particular, the Warm Springs were the last tribes to come into full-blown conflict with the Americans. This was because no one coveted their wilderness homeland until the great mining discoveries in the Black Range and the Mogollons in the early 1870s. With the gold fever came the bigotry and prejudice provoked by greed, igniting the last great Indian campaign in America. The Apaches when at war could be brutal and cruel but no more so than the Mexicans and Americans who wrested from them their homes, lives, and way of life.

The Warm Springs were finally brought to bay and forced to surrender and exiled for a quarter of a century as prisoners of war, not by the combined military might of Mexico and the United States, but by the shrewd use of Apache scouts. No one else could follow their elusive trails and track them down in the vastness of their wilderness strongholds.

As the Apaches waged the final struggle for sovereignty and the Indian way of life, we catch every now and then a fleeting glimpse of the most unique of the great Apache warriors, a woman named Lozen. She fought along side Geronimo, Juh, and the venerable Nana. She was the sister of the celebrated Victorio, who referred to her as the "Apache Shield".

In writing this fictionalized account of Lozen, I have drawn on the important work of Eve Ball in "Days of Victorio" and "Induh". Ms. Ball presents the most extensive record of Apache perspective. "I Fought with Geronimo", by Jason Betzeniz, is another Indian account which helps illuminate the legend of Lozen. With details on Lozen sparse, I have drawn on the exploits of other outstanding Apache women. Henrietta Stockels' book "Women of the Apache Nation" is a valuable source of information on the important role of women in Apache survival. Nana's raid through New Mexico is immortalized by Stephen H. Lekson in a study published by Texas Western Press. We know a woman accompanied Nana on this legendary excursion and, in my mind, it had to have been Lozen.

All Apaches were given powers by Ussen which were revealed during puberty ritual. Lozen's power was called "Star Power" and it endowed the recipient with the ability to foretell the future.

Apache Tears

About the Author

Tom Diamond lives with his wife in El Paso, Texas and he has a ranch in the Gila Wilderness of New Mexico. Tom is a practicing attorney who has worked for many years with the Tiguas in their efforts to be recognized as an American Indian tribe. He also played a leading role in the creation of Guadalupe National Park, and he has made significant contributions to the growth of El Paso including his involvement with the establishment of the route for the main interstate highway through the city. He has been active in politics for many years.

Tom's interest in writing novels began on his many trips from El Paso to his ranch. Driving an hour or more on a dirt road in the rugged, mountainous terrain gave him time to imagine how the West might have been in the 1880s. He began to create the characters for *Rimfire*, his first novel, published in 2004, and the plot and characters for *Apache Tears* while he was driving.

Tom enjoys writing and plans to complete many more books. He experiences a strong sense of completion and satisfaction when his books are published. He is also an entertaining speaker. Although he hesitates to talk about himself, when prompted he will discuss his stories with tremendous enthusiasm.

Book Publishers of El Paso

Order Form

Please send me (_____) copies of *RIMFIRE* at $15.00 each and

Please send me (_____) copies of *APACHE TEARS* at $15.00 each,

both by Tom Diamond.

I am enclosing my check (#_____)
            or Money Order (#_____)
payable to **Beaverhead Lodge Press**
in the amount of $_____.*

* Shipping and handling are included but please add applicable Sales Tax.

SHIP TO:

NAME:_____

ADDRESS: _____

CITY:_____STATE:_____ZIP:_____

PHONE NUMBER:_____

Mail this form with your check or Money Order to:

BEAVERHEAD LODGE PRESS
H. C. Box 446
Burnt Cabin, Beaverhead
Winston, New Mexico 87943

.